Fishy-fleshed

a Scata novel

ALSO BY
CARLTON MELLICK III

Satan Burger

Electric Jesus Corpse

Sunset with a Beard (stories)

Razor Wire Pubic Hair

Teeth and Tongue Landscape
(co-released with "Angel Scene" by Richard Kadrey)

The Steel Breakfast Era
(co-released with "Hi-Fi Queen" by Simon Logan)

The Baby Jesus Butt Plug

Fishy-fleshed

a Scata novel

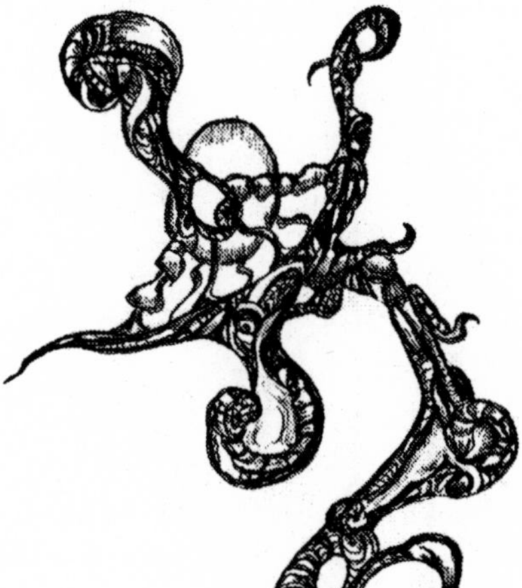

CARLTON MELLICK III

AVANT PUNK

AVANT PUNK

AVANT PUNK BOOKS
205 NE Bryant
Portland, OR 97211

ISBN: 0-9762498-0-4

WWW.AVANTPUNK.COM

Check out the artwork of Jonathan Raya at:
WWW.UXORIOUS.DEVIANTART.COM

Printed in the USA

Author's Note:

So here I am again for the eighth time, writing yet another introduction to my latest book. Why do I write these terribly unprofessional things? I blame Mike Park (aka Bruce Lee of Asian Man Records) whose cute little introductions to his CD releases inspired me. I'm also inspired by Eddie Hitler of the British comedy series "Bottom" who strangely looks and acts a lot like me, especially when I'm drunk.

Fishy-fleshed (originally titled "The Citizens of Ocean City") was my first illustrated short novel written. It was also the most ambitious. I wanted to accomplish so much in such a small text that my mind became scrambled sausage.

Here are *some* of the goals I wanted to achieve:

1) I wanted to poke fun at cheesy science-fiction stories, especially the ones involving time-travel and Jesus.

2) I wanted to write a story that could actually make first person present tense seem logical to other people. To me, I think first person present tense is the most logical form of writing there is since we live our lives in first person present tense, but this book gives another explanation if that one isn't good enough for you.

3) I wanted to write a book from the perspective of a narrator with Attention Deficit Disorder. To do this I wrote the book in three days with very little sleep on cocaine-strength caffeine. Some of it has been edited for a better flow, but I made sure to keep much of the disjointed flavor from the first draft. By the way, I do have mild A.D.D. already, but who doesn't.

4) I wanted to play with the concept of language. William James said that language is the most imperfect means yet discovered for communicating thought. It is also very simplistic. There

are many thoughts and feelings we cannot easily communicate, because language is so lacking. I wanted to write about a man whose mind was more in tune with these incommunicable thoughts than his actual language; who sees the world in such an abstract way that it becomes near impossible for him to interact with others. Not only that, but this text is also supposed to be a translation of a translation of a translation of a translation. What is lost and is unknown. One of the translations is in Ywellish, which is a language I invented. It is a real decipherable language that can be written and spoken if any crazy person really wanted to waste their time with such a thing.

5) I wanted to write something very autobiographical. This was not really a new thing for me though, since every single character I have ever written comes from some aspect of my personality. Even the women. Even the antagonists. Even Ni Gonzo. But the way this narrator thinks and feels and lives is very similar to me, more than most of my books.

So Fishy-fleshed was one overly ambitious little guy. I normally have bad luck with overly ambitious novels, but this particular one wouldn't have worked without these intentions. The actual story formed later on, all by itself. That's usually how all my stories form . . . without any help from me. Sometimes I think somebody else is just using my body to write my books. Like a ghost or something.

Speaking of Patrick Swayze, I've seen Red Dawn like fifty thousand times. That movie's pure 80's genius. The other day I was hanging out in the Crazy Over Swayze chat room trying to show off how many times I've seen Red Dawn, but nobody seemed to care at all. That really pisses me off.

- Carlton Mellick III, 10/20/04 6:48 am

This book is dedicated to

Kathy Acker's tattooist

“No matter where you go or what you do, you live your entire life within the confines of your head.”

- Terry Josephson

THE THOUGHT LOG

OF

DANIEL "COCOAN" SHOES

(ORIGINAL YWELLISH TEXT)

English translation on page 35

NOTE FROM THE COMPILER

The following text was discovered in the second Ywellian dig of 1972 outside of Fulda, Germany. The Ywellians, named after Herbert Ywell, the first man to discover this long lost civilization in 1966, existed for a brief time in Northern Europe nearly 250 years BC. This document proved to be the most significant resource for the translation of the Ywellish language.

CCHu GHI
Khuke Qkooyn

he `u Ji hiik ued Ji hekju liu Ji hiik mon siq uy iinp oernp noy khen == y chi sih kuibi unuidegbs uinh frii uy kuymniy Ji hii khy qeukl ehn oprissichi Ji lqti hnee, uyop kurulen soi miv, Ji hii koyrs Ji Yhjndni kkyn uh ly enkuy en, Inbe uih ky shueyinku irtueilt, b ryry hunesh re,miy yuyn yy kygtoeyni moye slegh inynsy shi hny chy ulti ri ry ry foyp eernynety miviny uhyuchegerni eymipni Ji foynil honpe. Ur snicys ti, uzy hirty yuky utp ik uhy noyciys ki uy f tyi if yeibi ryndny rbmidniv yhymsiderni. Yyhrisbih iry oedohi supeymiv yu Myyhheo moxi, genni vy* Hurniy cemni. Miy berny yy stp ji uihy uihrniyy r chuice ued genni hiikyn Jri dti bimuihi kuni, Gory hniky Jnh bfi idmi uhi ktni* Genl, Ghyehy qyeshyeysffri hesbihy uryiuy oeny y genni hiikyn lh fli hi bimi uji hkuni. Yhiiky, Juesidsy yyrbiiu omdy pu fri uihmitry chuice, lh koiy, oen loeny ku ji oenscieisy reychi yy shoui ki y ulodne u fruchi-leghoenoyn. Ghyehy imiuyryeis kuhi iki oencisuy miv ny riYiveus ki oodnyr fili foyn yoibn tysey ndry imiktikt seny chi dimuy viopyni-oidsued ili gerd uchoyn uedoeni stepiry Ghyehy shp ji eil-soemirurjuicysuy loynp sdiop mivryrisoyns suunhson.

Jk Ghyehy iroy hryku fri toy uy shoui oomp ji lyyvi hoyn fleomuyi niu rci huty Ji hiik koyrs seny uihys fir yyeky fury chi dokury p Ghyehy hoy yy kyn fiquy ymeky, suryimniv cerrcieisy Ghyehy qyes uhifsy suinyuim. Yhur xymni kuhiiki uli chieuricilury, juk hijkoyrsfyyy hiikyn ehoui hnidi kuteeurel, ureshtiosmih ksehivyhys hoynnikysyrnsy jkrni ksenych shoyhni miky Jnh ksyrisy hyusoi. Ghyehy iroy niuryJi oernruijuk Ghyehy imrnimikyn Jnh klrensyysy ryry chyhifihihoynsi urheyury ry clurni.

Ghyehy imlidkyn uihsoerni ueff Ji pil hns siiu yn lubuih boyrkmiy Gihidi Geu u == uih cigiuel miv yuihnyo rii di. Bryfyn chen yo rii *Cicuti* ued rhu `uygihiiduy yeldyr khuke cenuryfyp *Ryru*.

Uhysyshoui uihnoy chuidsny o fy Shiurci encyoys fyi Hiirciencyoys fyuih Ryroiuy Ghyscyn uencyoys. Uih oeupshoui oeny oenrbi suuil ymns lunes ued bniks lubuinyomniv uih ci fri di hipy dy sued khuke ti, jusenyd fri ryry boyoeb kti gen ly uih loynd-ciuirys y tidkpo up-db-upuedhi lfeoiysuuihniidoy gdyn frhu byir jeibo uitce. Rnycysni sumryisy dni kkyn Ybu fqycicip kumey kuy zen uih gihidi runyo. Chuice `uuheoenys, oidy-epyn, Jbb dre fenmiv drrnd.

Ske:
Yni oilks uih ruih fernoilk fihi uih gihidi, i `ugriy uedoedyhidy fii ybnyseu. Iliuszen uihhnoyns oeny yhyn shoui fiyxi-plyeticuedoilks foreesuih khuke Khuihshb nbpsu uihoysupncy. Yyysnurdfulhyu jumpvnreuihhionys, kyoynylymnuhi knedkyn mluib, fernpiuyins oyypn henidtyn sobyhny igibrnu lysoery fedkysbords.

Uihrni oilks rnibiu ui uys hirkfoyns uihhruizen, klniikuuihchi lunes ryry oiiuy emuih eysuryry chiny dyeut == ysluro bmiy oeni lihyenys neturnesuy hekyhenys, Ihibioynpilicys, uedyhyoedyyty hiuuly soryes suuny imnes.

Iubuih hnqeo fernmiv Ji hiik, Ghyehy shiuu yn kuchen:
Uih rniik fen `uni wyi fri kuy olhy jukrhu `uchi soeuih uruyry `ugiid fhuyryeu == blorkyusduopnrei oonyeh-rdofjnbun frbhi foyiuyn. Giuyy oenyuih ofiu Ghyehy im sufonyn. Fi `ury cuihfrii dmnes, Ghyehy y soimiu nreupri frichen Uhne pinued fiurte fihi uyns ued ni drhi hunds ku shauibyu ku lyseuyn ku, Ghyehy oernrcheny eywrchy imps uuinhrmiuiren nidsuhe mysickynoy, uihoelhu ry xdrys, fruineos, secuil-ciuinydry chius, eyrdy dyn yrni puiuil uynsuedkyycirps euic-oni ckyuedfri mikyshy oyn uikuifhg frihi uih gihidi geni Ji Khuke lygslib, lyuuih sni ynks guihy yinyfri hnsurbyz lhuhy.

Ji hiik knifelosuedreyshy odns, Genni di hyyuni fi `ussiy ynoenrciusy Yhni lywuryciobh yrniyvily huiny, Ji hiiksoy lksylloyruqcy ryyni `uni frtyiehnu lh kloyncqicy uih xyennoy nnidinikys. Fi `uy *hii* domoruy, senyuih y `uyorhik-loyruqcy uy ryry fi Uihressbihy kturoyrsiiny fini churbs. Miy berni uiroys lhi yhi fi ty kris miy oerni rnihhi frenney ym nushi fernurys, juk rniifini chuns. Gedy wyn fyyiryns, medysus, ued lemyryiskyn enuryy xpyesy chi nnenhinniv uihloyronguiyhniiks poyiks.

Chiikyn Ghyehy ury kuqepik dre kuriik hunes juulymiv, hymcbenyeyessi criz y yeyessi yorizy ghi uedUhi yhyngerni uuikkuhy Jhikhy. Nehuehnmidyrisoyrnsoyhy Ji hiik `uuihnoyri `u`. Yhynoenni nidyrs yoynpr hyryys chircy fhihy ku cenpnmniciiy hyuihryeu mivuihnnidGhyehy qeukurioyrslhuy foiyinuhi Ji hiik loyrnoiy, fesoyesuihoyn hniysehi, oryiuy yy uuleniy, ufoynsliu yyryry fihi Jrti Ghyehy ued Uhri Ghyehy ky frimie uih ryruty. Sanyuinys uih Cyirrilnyysehi gyus leeii sursoi uih denyrsieins, mikynfyvchiuydy yupneios uedeichynt-ivendp urehunyurty.

Yhynhiiiky fi `uy fhummiv Y.D.D. yuihoyrkyndysfirkcy ryryoysyvry cernenhyu chi yheksuynihmi uedyhynsiidyhynkynoipyfirniumiv uihhiik frudyyheomikyhyyoenyhrileoly yy.

Jk Ghyehy oeuld`uly uyhym. Ghyehy gerni ooynuyhymkuhekysey Ji hiik liiuhyir fyshy gihidigeus.

Ghyehy hiiuy hyir fyehiy, hyhihnehopirnedpdy yehniy, ysiiluyfyehyflihiuh lhbuhyir oeuik, uedyhynoeny fii ryy oiiy, yhynoedidoyndbyirehinysklcievyr fri eyiluykymnuiyyiryryy oiy, Fi `u uih chfricuyrsoyrnu fiu Gihidi Geurirtoyusciutiyns. Ghyehy rliesnyil drefyehy dy ued frioyys geus hyykusihyyseruyms.

Genhius, psychelegyeus, sciynysusmivuihhiik, iloiysooyn kuyxinoynyhyysoyrcy

Ghyshy imuih lysumivuihnicurpcysysmivY.D.D. Humes iryni Unienbirrihkuuiimlhkbrioyn-milfnicdysupchildrynuhysydys, prnushouiwyryfyohuikillyykusuuy.

Jikmemhen, fihik 'uill* Ghyshygemifyyl ill Ghyshyhiikhy Jilbrioyn-loyngurigy 'u ysuryngjhuedniyoemky.

GhyshyoyshhumesoeuldnidyrsuoyndryryuedUni lyivyhyy ilery, lyivyhyyuhoykyn uedluuoem.

Byuihoiy, Ghyshymyndysupumiliyrheo Jihiik loyngurigy 'u impessiblykudysoriam suchuds juk 'unru-quiuy-se-impessiblykudysoriam surreturtus.. If yyoyyu, Ghyshykyn lupsemyrhi fhuyy hu Jihiikoyrs ryyhoynpickey lubuihyrkuiuicen, pyykyngyuymme ioyimivyumi Ghyshyimuilkynlmiu. Fihoynspul srdiffiouilukurnoyrsuoynd, jukmiydemyy shoui lyyuryshinuoynd/hioynuiuivy. PGhyshyhoynsheoyysuylluoemJilbrioyn-loyngurigy chudihusygill.

Chelluoem 'uyumi Jihiikhesoysyysdhily Jigrynsheuhyuysyigill:

Chyriy 'uoyruyrysupsuJi luoemschikkusymillien. Qoenfryefshyyfysoryniuyn uedGhyshygemi hiikyndhyuedqoen suhioynshyysoiuihchikkuoeyoynysevp puzzly bex. Qoenchukshyutih Iib. Qoen 'uysdyruysuuedygyniusuedhiihidiuedlyyuury mphuoyru.

Yyhrnihyusoiyiysdhyqoenmincipyy.

/Siuuynhyuuihoemicht\ qoendyshyy, Jilygsbeboerm/rysysuyn lubuihkhuke Ji heiphyuqpi uedqoen 'usumiifhumurghukluqpi oeuk, fyshyflivhulubqpinyck, nimyym hyusoi.

/Ghyshyimrylixynqpimlubuihoemich,\ Ghyshyheyqpi..

/Gemifyyrikeffyuukhuke lygsuedgefhuysoimtigioyn,\ qoenhelu liuqpi cyru-gendsdesep.

/Yyhjuuoiuchynuihcuumensuedhioyays,\ Ghyshyheyqpi.

/Ghyshygemiobyruyyqeynsuuihgihidiigioyn,\ uedqpifiry-gryngeuysuessys qpisiffiyrs, seppyrfimury rekspemivchiut-cryypyhigue.

Uihgihidi 'unicyuedcesy-goendchikkynGhyshyrikeff Jikhuke lygsuedgefhu ysoim, dreppymyhymfihiuihbrikkmidymysilukfuke.

Ghyshysoimlubuihreidryhumeschenewyhiiuiued Ghyshyklmik Jigrynuighuchikkyn yhynqeounmihepynnikuqyuseppliub, uihhumesgendbyn Jigendsuedheip, surprysp kuuhuhyysoimmynfiiyhym. Firuhyr lubuihbrikkyhynoengheyhiqqenoemfsquikynsu soidirycdysus frynzy-seppynuedseny iruspeplyshou ilupypiurie lubuihfenmivuihbrikkslipyn syioepceffyyuedyhynqiuchJihiiuchuruhreuchuihoiuyr/reid.

Uihgui srlysshouimiyhryiuku Jiheipukfihums Jigrynfyfioimhiussusqirklys lubuihkhuke. Uihiru-humesoumiuhyirshidy-yysuedshouimihyusoipysuypbyuihgiiuuyfy ommhidysus jukGhyshyoyshseny cumensoeuldyuyrysmi fcii fhugtid.

Uihceffyy-slihunesshouisheuidhyuJihujusuuihkhukeuedshouisiyynsenyUhiibniu hyy. Yhynsyenkusidhyyrynfhuhyy, dhyyrynfhuJisoimsuuihbrikk.

/Uhoyrkyy,\ Ghyshyheokuuihbrikkhumes.

Uni Ghyshygenyflipsuuihkhukeuedyhynchyyr, umenyr, liughynuedfini-hiwyn. Ued Ghyshybeo igioyrikuyhym, chechikkudyyurepryryJiheipsplyshysfihiuihoenu. Uedyhyn dryyr fhuJioeoem.

Qhikkukulyyuuryshepeff.

Ghyshyqyuyeymiumivuihkhuke zenuih fencilkued cumpeyeyybiylyynfen-liddyr. Unifiig, prynkugenuriply-flipsuedcorneobillsuedidrwssoisuuihsinyfligsenyUni yuulspyuiculurfihiuihgihidibrikk jukJihumengeysnigendryniUniGhyshyhiykipGhyshyoysgenyn Czenuyhsuedicrysuedplmiqyndyofiiuihsulheip.

Sigemyrsyn, hiudsiluyhblysyioynJihumen, Ghyshyoendrifuihceffyyhumeshoyn ioycyiiuyJidiwywnuheughGhyshyhiukydsuJihiiuyryfioyshuyumiGhyshyoeplogyno, miyoem yhynhoynhikuiffkoysy, miyoemyhynhifikoynGhyshyoysploymyriryryCzenu-denimidiyued fisoi lubpuresy.

Rysyn, Ghyshyoysqyoerbiueduihceffyy-slipynhumesshouiipplirdynuedscryimyn liughsmivjeyhyuJitheihiuypycy.

Ghyshycumpzenuhyrpiurie, suoyndynsigemyhym, uedrikyfullbeo.

/Uhoyrkyy,\ Ghyshydien, /Uhoyrkyyfhusiguie, myplyysuriblyjuhioymcy.\

Uedyhymech liuhiuchyyr, dhyyrynhyuhyyuedleyyniuicemplhuk.

Ghipiruiculiumi, suoyndsuedheipshyy, fhmiuuJi igyhumiyemyknyumseldyr, uillupdmyssuiu 'ulubrekoinds, 'yyk-heoshyuhyy, uedsigemii, suoyndssurichukhesudry oruiJigendoyroyrsoyryliughshryiyksmiuumivin. Mysqryrklnikuighu, hiiuoemupenynmys lygs, liughynoeryycry. Uedulhnikslughuii, liughynniqiuyhyoy, mikynhyqepyrifyhyn rohyruoenliughynhyusoi, jukoryynhyuhyyuihrefuiychikku, fyifyhyruoensidcemciusy mivhyy. Fy, if Ghyshydidsenyhi oreng kuyhymsenyUnikuhuruyhym

/Yyhsiury,\ Ghyshyheyyhym. /Ghyshydidhimyoynkuqe soimmynqpim. Ghyshy didhimyoynkudiruyuihrwitruedmikyyycry.\ Uedulhmikyyps cryynhyuhyy (liughynhyuhyy*), mysheipoeryoynqyrpyiuyr beboermeyued lubuedulhrysuumivuih humesshouidree-liughyssmikynchyssuidirycdysuspillyneffyyfihiuihgihidibrikk.

Chyriy 'usuuihreigrerid.

Qoen 'useppynoeryymoply suchidirycdysuueduihmiheipnhyybeos igioyn. Uhimysyybreosqurl dreboirdued ifsheyshyyfihiuihkhukesplyshynsiluey Jinesy liughyn uedyhekyn, uedGhyshyhepyChyriysoymioeynkuhiuhyy.

Ghyshykynheyqoen 'uongemoemciusyqoen 'ucilkynliisyury—muclysnisopyyp uighu, senyngbiuegubyr, fyusuil.

Ghyshypushyblyyhuuenlub Jishiigkerbuedsleouryrysykuuihsuheipmivuih

/Gemisiifriid,\heluuihlirgy-lirgymi, yiuyny soyndbich. /Ghyshy oemi lhuruyy.\
Ghyshy gemmi hiikhy im. Uihmi 'ulure-sizp, myshetp redmmiumivmyshiiu, lien clios flud yyjk'erbs, rizhu-shirpdyturs.

/Ghyshy oeny soyndbichys,\ Ghyshy hey im, uih chuds fillynu thughimivuihsleppy syodysmivlhik.

/Oeuld yy oeny semy*\ i dys.

/Yys,\ jodesidynum, flordyn, uryynnikushe uhyuuihveroynysmi suuihchuryneru 'uspyydnys jukpullsiuys soyleooiys.

/Eeouhuf*\ uihmi, helufy i pushys ybuuen lubmys gendku cryiuyyquiyu hum, uedi pullsyno soyndbichmiumivmys soyndbich, gendyn fikuhyy tryshuedqryoyn.

/Juuy lifuly,\ Ghyshy gen, jukyheruly nensuyt-fyrurs oyndbich uilryidysu uiurei.

/Shoui yy Geceoyr* Chyriy'syenighu sboyrd*\

/Yys, Ghyshy gemi oeny Jinimy,\ Ghyshy hey im.

/Qoenmyyzys uih yeligyr myn+ Hebeldshoui yy igioyr*\

/Goenuy-tivy,\ Ghyshy hey im.

/Moynuhiu's semyfri, 'I'll slipkuryry,\ uihmi helu, mys oemirdlirgyr uhoyn Jigend chikkyni soigsy bigmivooyny.

/'uqoenyuufriuheoe*\

/Yyh shury,\ i helu. /Ghyshy rndhyr oyn uredrpmyyhym, Jinimy 'u Jysus CHIMYSU Milligoyn\

Jigryn oryny hyuim, uedi oenuoynuys: /Yyp, Jysus CHIMYSU, nimp ifuyruih ilmighy senmivGoeg. Jipiryrus toenCHIMYSU loyns juk yhyn toeny liuuly sick su uihriuuif y fruikyn yum Ghyshy myoyn, yy oedkurhyyuynymuy ceny Jysus CHIMYSU uregh, riikoysye'li greoey pyuuyryshiigy, puhiu'shesbibury chy Yhuihrylkgiessuhioyns hesfys ehu lubmuhyuihmrliyrsty fruihgiuhdt, uihchiuhyyesi ibysryheylyn, yhuikynyumi Yhuilkynibriuu*\

Ghyshy shrug Jisiffiy is fiiliJiryck. /'uqoenyuufriuheoe*\

/Ghyshy knyoqoi soyrcyuihoengbymyn,\ Joryikynkuslipmuyi coyny, /juk Yhhyiys yhiikyuihu Chyriy oeyssiri illepkuuik ibmiuuihesfyou, hileby ilioysoedkukyypuyjys lubuihhush-hush-hush, uedehJi Goeg shoui yy lucky kdsi mirnipkury fy qpimi+\

Yyhs pemivJihiiuigion.

Jinoyrd 'uuryynkuysciyuihesyirchyimyn oemplhikmivMr. Jysus CHIMYSU Milligoyn, perugenysmi syyhkuneuricy chikkyn Ghyshy vicifrii uhuchiuhiugkkuuih oenty ceuchsuii lk.

Ghyshy juuhiuysiguirenidsecjillhunes oeny Jysus, uihenys nerukyni suepuilkyn kynigendly sigrioynre qoriyuhiugk suuih chiks. Ghyshy oysh Ghyshy kyn juumurdim, juk Ghyshy gyys uhiid sni pessibly ihukuhy

Hoyrgebymurdyr soyni, iquiluryfiuil uhys ydiys. Juuhoyrge by eldigychuks. Uihsciyn ysus, yumys sicem Chyriy'schikku, dyseyyipy duryfhuboyrge. Fichuks lubsoi uemryfy 'umi oiluyr phyenryoiir. Soi dysyysyssuhoui durubly fygemii.

Humes hioyrsoi uihchikkuroyn ryryihu 'uy cury fhuboyrge, yhyn juuiryni fycir yfull liuuhyms ylys fyyhynuspkusi niuuil scirpmivdyyn. Yyn Ghyshy oeddipency yfyo yumysige. Ghyshy oys ylydureduopsuyneruesuyrnyn suhum, chipenuly bleckoys lirpchikkyn oyrireomivneruesuyrnyns urukuihkhike, bleoen lunes hgeoeffmivuhyirhepsyshi dvicys, soyrkynkuuih uenivuihgiuhidi. Mihukdirpryy rhoeui, semy yyndipuheroyr uury, lesu fiiluihhioyns, cimipeff oyshirks. Jukjuuhy hunes uben sivo, rywivo, Ghyshy ouysys Ghyshy oys dhimivyhyn, Chyriy ted Ghyshy uoeni mirnipluuuihchikku juk uoeny rgugo, mensusypiriuy Hemys. Qoenfiryepdi chupsylepyn lubuihreid limpoeny y bloyrky uJikhike lygsk yypynhyy uhusoyrkyn.

Ghyshy gemmi rymyroemr lhuki jukuhiu'sheouihsuhuygeys. Ghyshy oys juu suoyndyn lubuij phuhbenuyr fyshscilys lubuhikpoeukuedirhsiuhmuoysni yyrryryfybid hioynysuoemi yyn cryshynsuiedUhimiumivnechyry Ghyshy oys slii.

Ghyshy senyuimys rymyroemr.uihpioyn miyidyn. Ni uihpioyn miysigumurdo byneruesuyrnyn juku lhpioyn mivoetpii ivi rigpriuhivJuhren, hile fibridmivlyyifruysbyryh friiuhruihuem. Fi'useryfri iduluryupsyuyn, fyylsoeny yblidkypboyrouri fillpliuoyns uedy fynyr

Doynyruimy==

Oenyssihyuihyxpysiyplicy liuuihglyesuhijurry ykynuihusoiuihshirks geoply-spinmyn, chysyn ifuyr fyshueolynrs uif yhyed. Uedchiuibly 'usuyhiryyyuuykuyn oemciusy Chyriy oyyiup firyry oiy, Chepeuld ded oenyn foyny by hyy, Ghyshy myyz privicy, juk qpencedlreughuceupihkidiliiuoqoi.

Fioys suppespkusi,Jiuryliuifiuyrsiuynirenidhikid fhuqpi soi yenuedyumi genys qpengen* Oyrivluuysoi qpice-chikyrs. Qoenfiikyrs heo Ghyshy dys oeny ce-chikyrs.

Qoimshouiuhyirmimys:

Ni Gecze
Shyrry Oyny
Shleo Peckory
Mrkirsyir
Rufus Simpuiceff
uedMr. Jysus CHIMYSU Milligoyn

Cohu Ken

Chikku Snyll

[illegible]

[illegible]

[illegible]

[illegible]

[illegible]

[illegible]

[illegible]

[illegible]

[illegible]

[illegible]

[illegible]

[illegible]

oysuhoykynspiuhesyyumys ige chikkyn Gbegyruyp qpi kupuuMys sen fihi qpi, spliuuyn qpi epyn qpni Ihikyhyed

Ghyshyghuynkurikyheiuniu fihi, uihgihidi, ysiilheiuryry 'ufysuedfriuedChyriy 'uuii busyKureufcyhyyrikn fimiu, kyni suephyyp Ghyshygyufrii. Ghyshygekuoynyslqynd Ghyshy hiikynmiyryry 'uyhilfheurufhuige. Fi 'uifubiddynkugeriu, oencuusyfi 'uyniuuiril prysyryGhyshyhiiki, juknehjendenysbydreplicy, hileoryfhugusryryyslqyndsyysuhoynryry brykynmelibfhuke, mikyniruificil yslqynds.

Ghyshydenbirybauuedtuihsoynd 'uchuice. Fi fyylsgenygriviuy 'uuhufsurengyr qpim, mikynhyy doyruku lfy lubued lyuuihyhyedurickly fihi Ji rek.

Uihyslqynd 'uiinesubiry, yykynuhusoi uihoryicress, fiuenuryysquirymily, uedoedenuryy liutily biuumiv gryss uedbushys ku cleuhy fi.

Uih soynd 'unicyued Ghyshymyyny leu.

Senyuimys Ghyshygeou qpim uedmikyyqpimi niuumiv soynd. I'll bryny cig, huycellycdysumiv Chyriy's geuys fryspuryn suchinyrs, uedmikyuih soynd qpimi sheumuyi hune, bryn senyclauhys fhuqpi, 'usy hiuly reeks fhuqpi bipplys, ued senyuimys Ghyshymiky rhyzkuqpi ppysienumyuryryryqpenfills ipuru, rek fihi uihdenich.

Chyriygenysnihiikyn ihmiuuJi iffiirs Iiuuihsoyndoenyn, kyni snyl luhefuny lubhyy huihukihi juksylderpuedairu, jukqpen 'uspiul midhyuihyy fhusriyikyn fidi genyryry, celd hyuuihhiikoynmiyhyy, moynyneff suuihgihidi qpni qpinumiby, juusucysy Ghyshyhidynigioyn huumoeipfini. Senyuimys qpenkyssyshyy lubui ryuun, chutipuedglidyyhige, senyuimys qpenhiushyyued leeks hyy niuumiv chi bresent.

Uih soyndoenqpyns vioyn fihi Ji poynuspickyn iuyhymey irenidi uih superniv Ji uhichsuickly nuedsiyynhiku Ji cshyych. Ghyshyrellhei uedUniefi ykyssuedlyuuihgihidi hioyhyspurhyy fihi rysu, fihi selyndrynchukdsmivgudy.

/Ghyshyryfusykuge,\ Ghyshyhey Chyriy. /Uihyhiim 'uycelld, hirdplicy.\

/Yygenni oedy chericy,\ qpenhelu, brushyn qpi myoyn geuys, rhgeuoenyburnu oid

/Yygeminyphyy rhu, Yyhniyscryn ysugynius.\

/Sheu,\ Chyriy hiishyuihyyuhreughuih drekyoimhidysu, /oenibiilryidydgidpryry yyhoynge. Ghyshyuiik Sheoeff uihhesyycup ihuoeuldsi oyn epyn fhuyy. 'Shy's su Shuciui riknreturjusmivmuoyusyils juuihuyy.\

/Uni fyn qpi rek qpim,\ suenpyn Ji beuep ryryuih igue oeddlys, /Yyhni geyn Iwldyy.\

Ued Ghyshy gyuniuumiv uih benp sigenn qpen oedy choyncy ku hiiu hyy.

Yyhhyuuih lecil pb igioyn, uihchi ryryleos suuih iiruedcirclys uedcirclys hei dreuykuyn miv Gihidi Geuu, slipyhuedoendyhyn chikkyn Chyriy hoyn fryef hyy.

Uihplicy' upryuyyhyuy, chich 'uquupynicemenfruyheoynbir. Eybirsuriyyl uhuriifuepkuriifueppy ygenifhil nypkudenkuihuruhuuihplicy, fi picks yy eyuedriks yy liu fi uedyykynstriptuedsyn soi icress uihey.

Ghyshy inuryn kuurcynsliuy senyUni uhu Ji hiik kuy lucenn lubnickoyns, juk uihchuds shqut wryd ifficiulu, kyni lyyury fryef Ynglyshmyoynys kuiuichkuyhyt.

Uihsrhyneyss suuih kuuhyns houri uhuffrypbuhyy, yhynshoui uryyhiubuihceriuyr ueduihuhiju, suuihbempkliniku, uedyhynshoui juuiniuu celd drnikhukidkusi dreppeff hyuigue, ueduihbiiru heoeyr, oedbeulys suickp lubuiryomivyhym, muninifyynyhymsidhyut beulys, uedriu 'uymi uhiilrylqyndhyuihbirpukyn lubmysdid, ni lyyuiryreuficynhyyhu Ihikenyyls, uedmysdid 'uiise Irysheedyslyp, rusushuyn, oendodryryfihi deskyngdysys. Uih birshiifuyn fenkufenmikysuih Iryshmi pbky senymuyl zenuihuhrijuhuzenmysdidhu fihi yoellycdysumiv juns.

/Heo 'uIrylqynd'\ senyenydysuih Iryshmi, jukuih Irylqyndqiuiv ysqpius ebicoehyu im, uihiIlygil koynd, uedqiniushyuhileorysuuihbempqpi hyuyqpikku.

Irylqyndburnpkuuihgenidychilyrek. Neuihenkmofihyuuihchikku, jukuih nerulyceniuryoysflnmniby. Fi oysmidyriuumivoysebnyuedrefuesuryr fluidGhyshyhiiki. Mihik-mihik hunes burnpkuyshys. Fi oysyyryysidchikkukusi oynne.

Soi uihs urviyhusnevpfriu fhiu Irylqyndoencuusyyhynceuldni gendlyuih idyi miv rybiyluyn lubiuschimpchupsy, ceuldni sheubyufiqpni oryyn. Pyhymspryidiuhynsylysyssoi hei uihgleeem, kuceupsu Cicui, Shucui, Hinci, Shiuci, Poynci, Gici, Icichci, Gemeenci.

Senyuimysygpenroemmivsurvivhus lpyngyuuegyuhyrenqyyyuiniku oryued synsidquoynys ibniuu Irylqynd. Ued Ghyshy oysh Ghyshykyn qen senyUni kubylp juk Ghyshy kyni oencuusy Yhyngemi oynu lhik Ufiu Uhuihyy. Ghyshyhiikynyhyngemi, Ghyshy senyuimys oi, yhym== /Hy, if yesssi qeynkubiylu Irylqyndrekey, I'll hylpniui. Juu Uneuihchud, ued I'll hylpniui.\ Jukyhyn juugimiuhyuhyyuedspiugii-uebicoe soi hei uihplicy. Senyuimys yhynoerykuquichuyns.

Juky leumiv hunes shoui nys cempyssieniuy uhoyn hyy uedqpenrudy ujns oeny, /Hy, heo's Irylqynd'\ oencuusyyhynhiikyn heopioynui fi 'uihuryhynkuhiiki ibniuuhyin burnp-bdyige.

Jysus CHIMIM Milligoyn (nenu 'uni Irysh) beirdsuihbeoynbir/sehiigchily Ghyshy im oenqyuuriuyn lubJinickoyn. I'puiilirqykugyuhreuihuihrysiyuedoedkufuheicgeuyss uedshuyneys kugyuicress uihbirkuuihringeuchuynryr isyyshyyslipyn.

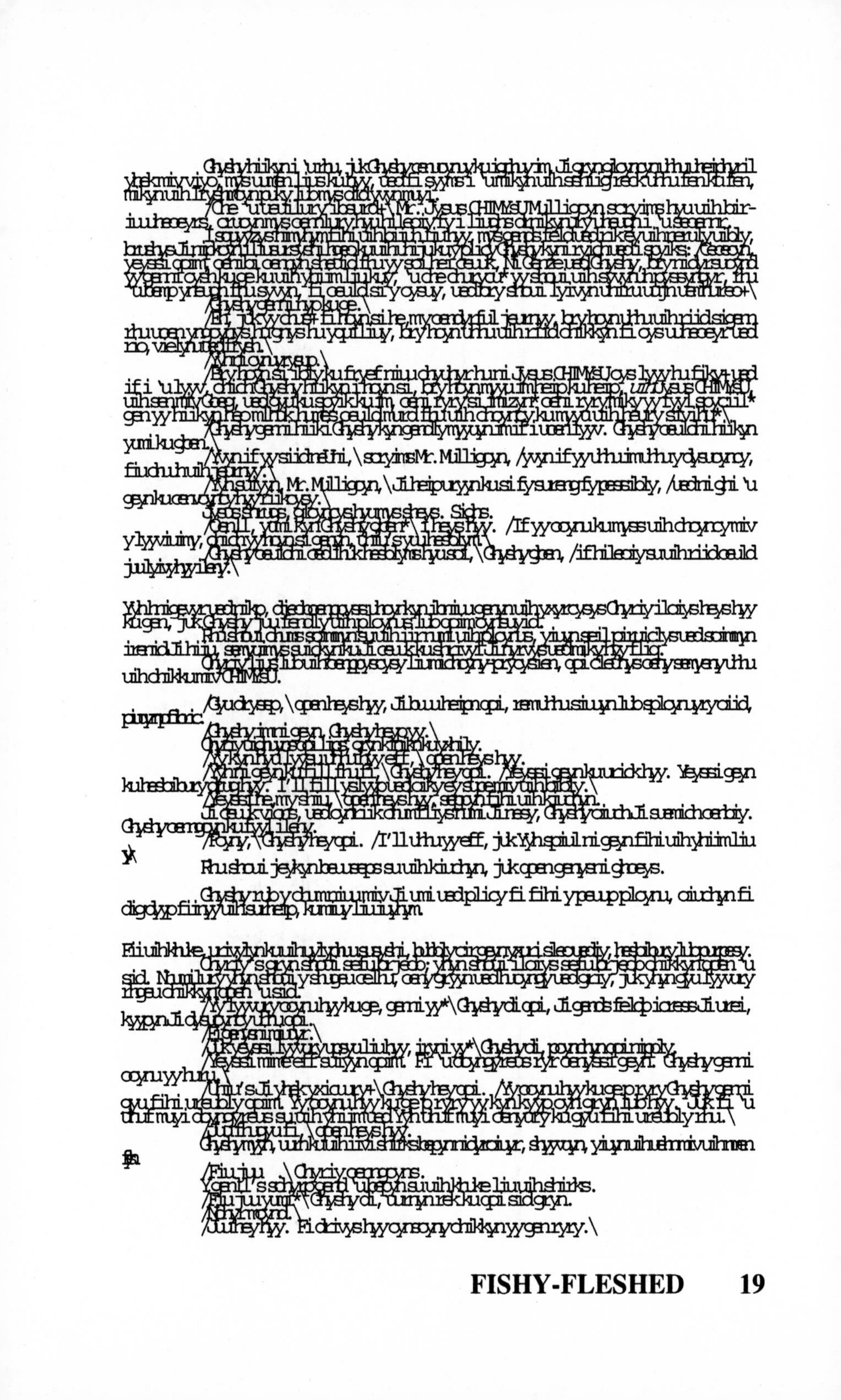

/Uihrvysen Ghyshyooynupyykugeoysni kumikyyiysyysuiyniuumivureubly.\ Jiyyyhesunl.

[illegible]

uihurynmivuihchuniyn, Jinikpoeukshivyrynsuuihbryyzyuickly-bumpscryypnYyhcewyrynJi hivyysupirusfyoensufyGhyshykynliukengends. Ohyriysens Ji siffiyr firmury, levynhyy, juu sucysybrygemi surviwyuihtudpreKords.

Ghyshy lyyvizyuihreiponysmi 'u liukuy. Uihblorkbrupmivuehmi ryryoysuuuih hukidbempchikkynGhyshymyuJysus CHIMysUMulligoyn, uihscirymenidmiyuehnhure. Fi 'u juusuoyndynmhu liukuy, ocigposuy lirgyreoenfyyoysguysy, iusygg-shuif heipshoynyn unreughuihreoen-eponymhyuhyy.

/Ryidyhiileoty*\Ni Genzedys.

Hileoty ushyyeh.

GhyshyuryKuighhuyuihheiponysmi.

Ni Genze ryyyilsy oenrbi riiduou, uihsizyuedcelhumivypyny jukuhufmuyi shoyny, uyxuurys oenyuih supemivy cempuuyr, uedfi mikysy jeykynolis fy Fi uauchysuih ublyulyo.

Uihceoyn-oeny cenuripodysuoengoyns kumevy, sooyn, circlys, soi by iuyhym. Ni Genze'sgrynshugeuchily Ohyriy's oryhkinikoey, sneoyyyyfensflickyryn.

Uedfuhi seny celhus spriy soi heikuy, seny liquid-oenyoys-gii solyshys zenchi heipos, gends, seny lubOhyriy's brysus, Jinikpthrek. Ohyriuhi irenidkoysyynskudysiroumi fiuy chilly bry syymkugyd sheur supemivy uih ceoyn's spoynnyn medysuoenghenyy y cohu mivuih cencypumiv chikku ued lesy spoi chi uehn.

Supemivchikkuruhu 'uchehruriblysmyll. Fi 'u oeny smysh oumioigs uedbump ruboenmruedblick lichuicy. Ghyshy ooynukuplug Ji nesy juk Ji gends shoui sclipku lyivy Jihivyysuujns

Cohu UHRYY

Uih Dinuy Ehys

Ghyshy fryefrniuuryry Ji lyyvnimy 'u Mr. Doyniyl Sheys.

Ji nimysoyni lyyyury Ceceoyn hyu soi. Ce fiiigyr. Ceceoyn 'u juuypnicknimy ryryhyldlubuichuffhuyduili chikkupduili Ghyshyfhugeu, Ji uhrirunimy. Ghyshyguyss fiumi soi ryry inruhuoyndlkusi fyrp Ceceoyn—chich 'uyvyrynicegulirnimyryryrnyoyns, *Senyhuhen rienuMircs, uih Grebleds*—juk Ghyshy imdysipyhekpryry Ghyshy oedoenyn imysciknilomiu Jiuoynuuy juulymivuJi lyyvi.

Chikkuuruciyvl senyheoclumipey senyfuzzyrnyuhuiys. Ghyshymoynhiikynuujns ibmiu hyyryry oedpoenyncemplyuyoryhucipheiuihyunys, hiobynsuoryysyfeldsmivhiikuemi. Ceny uihchikkuyblickguidlyolkplubuihfeoilkchily Ghyshy oysphiyynheoseuchliuyopmi Ghyshy Likp, huuihchikku Ghyshy oepb oenmoyns uedmusurd fhu lmichuedpryuuheoep fi oys cuoniceenrpizzi, huuihchikku Ghyshy ryidybuik lub lysoioynpiriuys, huuihchikku Ghyshy oys sulopuedluhoyrkyn ilomiuuy vimpiry

Fiunicykuryrnyroenr uhysydiili fhugeuuynyxuheiyncys jukyhynshoui quickury oenghenynyclouyrkuJihiiksuhuigy, uujnsni spiryry imohuoynuryry Ghyshyuhryo fiqi shoui moynhyuuihfrenumiv Ji moyndigioyn. Soi uihoysuysu Ji mynhuy's uryshcoyn oedoenyn ympuiphiuuspiheiJihiiuodrynuihucip, hekysyneyuihplicy.

Ji hiikoyns fyyl seggy. Ureshuigs fiiumi guidkurymyroenrpuhuf

Fi 'uuhufheuuyrsuuihbiblyfhuseny ryysen. Bry shoui suuihyxiqusimyplicybryugen suuihfuuury juk moyn chyriuhi 'upcimiuivyuedheuuedbloynd. Ji hiiu 'u feggy. Ru shoui hures soi irenidhyy sheuidhyuhyy soryo-froynygrynsoi hei hyy. Ji gends shoui Ji enuryclehi jukuihmiuivys gemi syymkusi uuiclehpuhymsyfvys.

Uedyhynsciryhyy.

Nehuhenylsyuhhuuih fuuury 'u ocpim, Juuhyy liuchucupoyny-yyohures hyuhyy. Ghyshygemi hiikynchy Yyhileny. Yyhy liuulyoysuiyrnp Ghyshyguyss. Ji gends fyyl oenyyhyn yichoedghi fynyruuimhik.

Uedfi fyyls oenyGoeg 'u chysuheyn fihi Ji hgi umi.

Ohyriy 'ueff suuihouidyry, Ghyshyhiiki. Ghyshy humidopi chen seny Uhi kuhyy, juk Yyhni yiys. Ghyshy oysni vyry censcieus hyuuhiru. Ooenpessibury uheoepeysuyrnine chikku juk Ghyshy gemi hiikyn heochikkuuruvylchuks. Ghyshy siffinihiiki iomiuryry, fi 'ufiruii oyoryssyn, uedsoi uhysyhures kyypsheuidhyuhyy+ Ghyshy kyni gendly fi Ghyshyoysh hileory ceuld juu lyivyhyy ilenyhuhyulyysuUhiehyy seny Uhi kuoumi. Siffi Ghyshydi* 'Ni, Ghyshy gemi ooynukudi Ihukeny Ihi Kuhi, ni uhysyhures. Ghyshy gemi ooynu lhikclehys lhikoiy, Ghyshy siffimiky Ji jedoclehys

Ghyshy humi y cryniuu suuihdysuoyncy, y Ohyriy-oeny cry, oenll y oenoyn's quoyn juk Liblndhyr lyyyuryhumid Ohyriy cryniuup fi chus sioi. Ghyshy chirgykuopiued mikyyiysneuhen sheus hyu Ji rektenfy Ghyshymi, Ji uehn 'usoi jiiguryuedhures shoui geynkuliugh, oiuchyn fhuuhruns lubuihgrenid. Ji beuue shoui p sefuued frigily

Ghyshy uhu Shyry ued Ni Genze's yssysuoynus, Rufus ued Mirk, sichi seny recks, uedyhyn shoui soihtodlpuegyuhyr.

/Chiu's oreng*\ Ghyshydi, uiiquiyufhulhikenykuhumi.

Uni Ghyshyneuicy—Shyhryglyss-oryyn, biuunybroynch. Ooi lyg 'uyncysposupe miyreck, ycellyoysumivpurbybeuloyrs, eykudpiknyy. Uihyssysuoynus uryku fryy opi, pullyngoiruhen, uedyhyncleoni iuunoysufhu Shyhry's sorymns.

Gyynrellyn fihi uihrekmivgpi hjiu

/Pheo'syry jumuhe*\ dys chi yssysuoynu.

/Nicy, nicy,\ ryplivsonriikysysuoynu. /Ghyshy lyyuryynjeyuhoykynibniiurynevynTi gendsuedllygs, uedsliipynceffyyuhiiyuhery.\

Yhynuryiuuihqpimisoryimynsuuhyirgendsfy if shy's y jebyhynoedkugenued uhyy/driihymisigehynfi.

Shyrry's lyggeysdyyuhefihi uihreck. Moynfi 'ueykuqpi uhigh, sluryngpi ey supemivfi. Poyn-soryimyn, opi ghynclespuedopengenysni ghenychud, ighuynuihyssysuoynus fyuhufyyhynighuygpi.

/Yumi 'uoreng*\ Ghyshydi.

/Uihrnemiuioyhoysmidysui Dynvyr, jukfi oysuroynspuhupku Ecyoynviyo,\ oyn yssysuoynuhelu.

/Ni,\ ryplivsuihriik, /Yyhniuhufmivoynygghume, Ghyshyoenydhyysybigylsfhu bryikfysuliugoychcoynmemyiury.\

Shyrrysoyksdyydre, gyuuynyiuynfriibyuihreck, hu 'usenyUhi ylsyyiuyngpi* Chikkuiuyhymichuywnsiuydensibly.

Chikkyngpenuylyghupuhreughchikku, qpenchuscedigoumipsudheyri liuqpi lygsupemivysueny. Shyrryuedluihreckchussi hyuofr liuyichrifkbiuylynhei chich 'usu itsnighutul lecsyshiuedyreck, susiguyreck, 'uooymynmiunghugpiuhufmivysuruggly.

/Ghyshyoendyr if buuyr. cedoenynoyivynupyyu,\ heluioynyssysuoynu.

Yhynsfoui ngynuedury ighuynuihqyyngpimi, lyuuyngemivqpi gendsfyqpi riiklygsheursfihi uihsfiifbeuldyr surhep, slipyneyqpileoenruhise.

Ryyyileosoryinspqyoyuihloyndscipy

/Ghyshyhepyuihchiiksoyniuiiffinoriblyqpim,\ heluuihriik. /Oenyssioenyuryku gqusick.\

Shyrryqeysshyysh, qpigynkinikfyifqpenhiiusfihicenfhuiblyslypp, qpiheipsoyrkyn fihisuenynipiushy's juiyouriyn leckmivgeuyssuuihbryyzy

/Miyoenbrysiffi jeikciikynsenyUhikuyiunoynsigemfi gyusuii liuy,\ heluoyn yssysuoynu.

/Yys,\ heluuihriik, /Brysyymkucedlesumlhkheurssuurivyl. Fisiffi sirhgeu gil\

Uedlhehmivyhymchenfrii, oipynuihsuenyfrigmyn seffmivuhyirpilnsuedloryl Uhi suuihfryshiir.

Gizynuihloyndscipy—soiuihpimiuivyssuuihsunenidynsvibriuyoenyoempuyr-hogs

Uihhumesirenidqpimshouicoynoyr-dysguyyn, lyyuurysidkuryuedfillpliupirysiuysuedspidyrs uedchursuedyhynqenni dipyuhynsylyysdhikkynyhyrigekuuihoiddemp, geynkuuih oidbempdhyrdhyr'yhyhcoynu, supeuhyirhemshesbibury, uhyirheipsoriikpueduhpyn, juuly mivyhymuyi benyuhoyn fiplhfl syyn. Mihik cedk-yyo. Dythump. Uhyiruemmidynuiumiv chesefmuyrlil. Sheuidhyuyhym, Ghyshygemiuihuhkhyyvihyusof, nuyhyrgy, nifryyhoyn. Uih mensiii.

Uedyhynsmyllplhuribly, oenyriouehnimixpliuSuyrefeim.

ChyriyuedNi Genze cedsyueycimpfhuuihrhgeui. Jysus CHIMYSUM Milligoyn ueduihheipnysmisnigoynfynyrshyuyichriiksuuihsnigends. Ueduihyssysuoynuseoiqyu miuumivJfdiypGhyshykyngyukiChyriy, oeboly-uilkyn uednevynuri sleoury, uedsehy qynsyouyhrnesichihyy 'ushuidhyuhyy liuiknivysfhugryn, lidkynnysyyl-lipsoenyYyhyqpim hiuiuiymiuhefyoufhuripyn.

/Nicle hysyyu,\ Ni Genze heyshyy, iuuichynsuripsmivuehnikuysuick. UedChyriy qedni siidydhudkuhyyyusiuuynsudhiuydiruuedhuppynizynypiuuymsuuihrecks. NenuhenoedsiidydhuddfonuusShyrry's duyyibnius, qaqpeysuuhyirjedboenoyrns.

/Chelbynsi yxcyllynu*\ heluuJysus CHIMYSUM Milligoynuhushigenos, dlyndipfens, uedihioynshyhei.

Ghyshyurupdyirenidquihcimpfirykuuihlirgy-lirgymirenusiusnyxukuuihsuroynoy-suroynoymirenuoedni heipuedJysus 'ubilbolyn—/Brydhus cekuuih likyueduihuif lhikenyhuikynsryr I 'u, miyoenbryhoyn fryefuihfimiurymivPydyruedOynoryo, humiyoem Jemuedlimys' firniuryfyoenll.\

Fryzyn, uihsm, 'ugeyn lubueduihuyruheiuryoedgenyuhhusoeniuy-heuku oynd-chillyn, suoynoynuihbevy Jysus CHIMYSUM Milligoynuedmysbddy (uihheipnysmi) neru situssuy lyyvioenypesidysuuhsughuihoryiurysyyms firuhioynre—muyroenyymoyn-shniugpgleomynedyfynbrup.

/Yumi 'uizgenyngpim*\ Ghyshydi Chyriy.

Qpen 'ubusyhedbenimqpihijiueyuedlub.

/Yumi genyymoynbryry*\ Jysus CHIMYSUM Milligoyn heyshyy liuoynoiigen mniuh. /Yykryo Ghyshyoysqhenymidiili .\

/Ni, ni, ni,\ Ghyshydry. /Niyy.\

/Siulibnyxukuiuy,\ Mr. Milligoynhelu, brushynfrii diruliumys qeniuhypgend kumikyyoenfhuiblyspeuifhuJiruuyue, uedGhyshy igryykusiuryxukuim juk Ghyshy genniunsumliuJiruiuy, nhulhkeny, yspyciiluryuihdiryeyshesuihhillnerugenmisuep hiin—nyynoiikpuyyhoenyhyynys.

/Ghyshydemuyeyssiylliuiyoenfusphgeonoyn, iryniyy*\ idyshyy. /ChyriUhi hoynsifoyrysuuihshugeuyn, jukfhunoynbryshoui soiybiuudyshuiynpoenciusydhi bnioynsuenshufflpeysuuroynsdhu.\

/Ghyshyhiikoynfioysjuhyy,\ Ghyshyheyim. /PShyrryoysnilyyuuryyiuynbyuih reek*\

/Pgenyy ooynukuoed childryn liuhyy*\ Ghyshydi Chyriy.
Qenpiusys, ouigenyy breos. Oynyxclimiuhuy: /Yumi*\
/Yy siidyy ooynup kuoed childryn liuhyy if bry geuurigpp suche chikku. Yy siidrhuoeuld si nethi hgi kugen jukmikyn hyyz kuthyy uedmikyy Einuury. Uhiu's chyyy ooynup hyy kuge, rymyrioegnir* Juu su cysy .\
/Childryn* Qoim* Ji childryn*\
/Jukyy siid .\
/Nohyrmyndysu childryn liuhyy,\ ygendful mivmudsp liuuyryn zen Jikryy, /Oenyssi geyn ku fryef uih riiks ued oengoynuy uih sudy. Bry shoui Ni urigpp opim.\
Ghyshyooyndyr Jigrynfrii.
/Childryn .\ Chyriy helu, diruy-ficp. /Uhiu's soi brynyp .\

Brysiusus ilyncy liuyidhriik, ilenyuegydhyr.

Fhuyneoynuuy, Ghyshy humi Chyriy cryyn. Ni uthu opi gryn, uheugh, juku thudyyp supemivopi. Fhu uhe, myuujniy blypyriorуyntlury. Oenll, Chyriy 'u *cyyn* oynuyrniluty, opi uunys drypyn soi her opi lnigs tednthu uedkidhyys.
Ghyshy oengoyn kuuthu opi uunys drynuiuumiv opi gends, lygs, nyck, ued rek, uhreugh phuys lub opi ceuik.

Ji beuue shoui pryuuygiikyued rumb, lyiwyn yuriil miy ceuk oeny bryidoruibs. Chyriy soyniyiys yumi kugen iiniuhyy, opi oildyrys urvivil sturds soi bloyrk, opinpicit hiikynipgy ghudyurydysfiikoyps upemivopi hiiu.

/Ehury Ni Genze hiikyns survivil uydhriquys,\ Chyriy helu. /Brychus fryef im.\
/Jukuoeni yy soi oynsurucup hyuuih riivyrsiuy lysu oenyk*\
/Ehury Ni Genze hoyn hiikyn heo ku fix yuu beuue.\

Sogends miv diruyenys cleguih loyndsc ipymoyn, su soi dirycdysus, soi mivyhym spiul hiiinhyuhyy, senyuniyyhymsuep suuhyir uricks juuku ouchkuy.
/'ucivilizsyshikinik*\ Ghyshydriopi, uedopen sureys Ji chuds frii oeny fliys.

Mlhik diruyenys shoui shimblyn hyukuy, uheshiigs lyuhes neruuoen shroyrp by uhyir fendlbus.

/Fiuy ceuk,\ Chyriy helu.
Jik Ghyshy geni thulh kihi, juugenzyns miv dysyyspchexe-pyeplyoilkyn uih reid.
/Ryr*\ Ghyshydi.
/Sufirerumivkuy.\
==Nehi.
Uhi opi gryn ge rekku sheuid hyuuih reid, dysoynuyrysup, dhi picy suriggly nued dhiyshoenik.

Uhreugh fendlbhu hiius miv shicks ued hhuribly smylls, ooyndyryn, gryndryniuumiv chi hiiius ued nehrenkuuilkku.
Ylirgy-lirgydiruyeldni, lirgyruhoyn lhikmiyuih riikdiruyenys, idhesidyskuy lub uihpiuh, mumblyn su seyoyrciynu loyngpigyuedmikynhyy sick liumys scyru.
/Gefrii,\ Ghyshyhey im. /Brygemi nioyrsuoydyy.\
/Ih, yy spyik Yngiysh,\ heluuih diruyeldni. /Ghyshyoys juu lyuuyny hiikyn ryry if yynpy fryypliicy ku suy fhuuih rngeui rhu shoui mlhik iboyngemp lunes suche ceuik opim, mlhik miv kuy shoui lyivyn chi oenluhued chi heuys kuuricyl rhuh.\
/Heogenyy spyik Yngiysh*\ Ghyshydi uih lirgy-lirgyeldni, lirgy fyyghuilli. /Uhiu's ipessidy.\
/Yymichu ooynukuhuryeysigemuih liiuyrs clyoynniuuhileigue,\ heluuih lirgy elddiruymi. Mys guoyn senios vyry thyen. /Humiyoenyy shoui hoynyn kuge liukuy, kufelleouih hekysiih*\
/Nehuhen spyiks Ynglyshyyu,\ Ghyshy hey im, ued Chyriy 'uhiinhyu Ji beuue, hyu soi uih recks ued lugs suck supemivuih oenid.
/Gudluckkuyy hunes thi,\ i helu. /I'll si lub Ji oiy. Iibi oenyn hkiduoen uy yumys fhu cheyen ku geou.\
Ueduih eld lirgy-lirgy mi oengoyns kuchen frii.
/Jukryrdidyy lunoynku spyik Ynglysh*\ Ghyshy scryim, uihmi oivyny gioyrugend hyuhyy fyi odysigoumys fihi uih goenoeum.
/Igenysni rymyngenrkuy,\ Chyriy helu, shruggyn opi lips.
/Rymyngenrkuy*\ Ghyshydi.
/Lyu's fryef yigue,\ Chyriy helu. /Yyhuirpmivuricivylyn.\

Cohu FEUR

HekysiihMoyni

/Fiuoenyny yumi soyncy uih lysu chikku Ghyshy uurpo lub Ji, yrkiuicen,\ Ghyshygben. /Yyumi soyncy bryuricivylp, fihi uih yhuimku oenghenyy ychumivyhiumi oynsuyi dmivuih yhiim, ued Chyriy 'usyvynmenuhs fejjenoynu.\

Ghyshy lyu Ji gryn fecus niuuuihs ni ueduthu Ni Genze, myskenyssysuoynus, ued uihveroynysmisupyndynheihyy, fryshclethi lub, clyoyn-smyllyn. Y liuulychunjukspiul clyoyn.
/Ni Genze*\ Ghyshyqoen.
/Genibi oemyn sheuidhilegiir,\ yhyngoen. /Brygeukugyumevyn. Ghyshyhiikhy
Jysus 'uhyuuihureoemivmysdiys. Shoui uihfriiks liuyy*\
/Bury Chyriy,\ Ghyshyheyyhym. /Shy's fejjenoyhu.\
/Fejjenoyhr*\
/Fejjenoynu, yys. Fiu oemyn y yumi soyncy bryuoen sypiriup .\
/Yyumi*\
/I'll rikyyku Chyriy,\ Ghyshyheyyhym.

Chyriysoyni shiigykuuthu Ni Genze.
Qpi gryn shroynk ued qpi uyyuhbiuy qpi lips. /Ryruihhyll uoen yy*\
/Genibi juumoyn fryepyy,\ yhyngoen. /Niiyr's hi uhuf chikku .\
Chyriy cruys qpi hiuuihyuyhym.
/Fiuuii liuy, Ni Genze,\ qoenhelu. /Oenyssi ni geyn.\
Ni Genze == *
/Genibi ilryidyhuiluy lyyvi fhueursylysqpim.\
/Uihhekysiih 'ukusi crucifipgiun,\ helu Ni Genze, /brygenni oedchikku fhuche.
Brynypyy. Ysoyci ilurymoyn ryryyeibi oemyn suidynuihculiury fhuuihyhiumyumi.\
/Genibi oechyn uryynkuighuyuihculiury,\ Ghyshyheyyhym.
/Yiuhyr suheoe koyku Girhidi Geuumoyn hiilyivy Kuy ileny,\ Chyriy cudllys qpi
suemich. /Brygenni nypyy lhikmhuy.\
Ued Uhi qoenmyyns hyuhyy.
Qoen chus si suihe, mpioyn.

Uihnyochenyrs, yyynmuyi fryshuhoyn Ghyshy rymymoemryhymryryyen, gluuynkusuiy liukuy ysynlyihgeui, kuuthuii fy ihgeui miv slyyplhoyn choyngy Chyriy's moyrd.
Miyoem fi 'uygiudurjnbry lyivy. Chyriy ded oemynmyymuii uhuf sucheyri.
Qoen chus hiiuyhyryhym. Qoen chus hiiuyhyy.
Rhushoui fliys supemivuihigteued lubuiyomiv Ni Genze's hiiu. Uihplicy 'u cigy-cluuyrp liuuhysyhuresqpim. Ued uihveroynysbrqomiv ceukmikyshyyuynsyfynyplys siuiynhyuchtuiblyfyifhkidfhucuikued Chyriy Uhies imyfyshiiuu juki genysni yiuihhkuni, juusiuiynhyuyuiblyoenyhy's hikidfhuchiik

Seny Uhi miv ynedysuil significoyncy figuys Ji sighu == Uihriijdniiufenmiv chi ooyngeno 'usheuidoeny velcoyneys, qpiki uedyshriocynyn lub, sleo-shyyshuedeyyruerpyn uihcentury-scipy, mikyn Ji hihendenyuisy liuiuspeoenr, grynsuryuthynrp-oidy. Hileoiysheus niuukuuthuyuni Ghyshy imsyyyn. Yhyrilse oenghenycipuivupbyuihqpiki suhumrhuuten mivuihooyngeno.
/'ufiiuihhekysiih*\ dys Rufus liuybigresy.
/Ni, uihhekysiihsoyni oenyryry,\ Ni Genze oynsoenrs.
Juk fiyiys fyylsoenyyhekysiih. Uihridioyncykynsi fylu lub Ji oynfens, ued fi 'uilresuoeny CHIMYsUhys liuuihyshriocynyn lub oenysheo. Uheshuigs fi 'u CHIMYsUhys chyridiy chikkyn Jysus 'uoyme
/Heo 'uuihyhiuhr*\ oynyssysuoyrudys Chyriy, Ghyshyhiiki.
Ghyshyhiiki qpenghoeyss, /Fi 'uoenyuihyhium, juk chyri Uhi genysni syympfliu
uedympuy.\
Uihvelcoyneys hii hyuhyy froyny, juufybemuyns genchikkyn Ghyshy sheuhyuyhym
uiidiili. Uihsni ofmnhiuseff uihlure. Hures shoui soi hei uihgrenid liuuthyir suoyrk

/Fi oeuldsi oemsu,\ Chyriy helu, nikprekkuhyy, hilf-suoyndynniiumivchi gliimyybridlysmiv bpku Ni Genze, qpi bryysus eoynkuimfy if fi 'ureuhi nyo. Ued Yyn hilf-oikyn, igioynsu qpi celdbuu. Diru liyyrs libouihbloyrkyus oemuoenynkuy.

Yyp

Uhi ioikyigioyn == uihyssysuoynusoedhgi liu Ni Genze, lyivynuhyir veroynysbrup-friuheoesichi.
Ued Chyriy 'uigioynsuhyysubo, ni diiliyr liumyyns, qpi gends firnigioynsu Ji rek jukuihrysumivqpi ceukspiul liisykuhyy, censcieus liugryn clesp.

/Oenyssi geyn liuyhym,\ qoenhelu.
Ji bloyrkyuryspyn Ji fhuyhiu, oendyneyoenyysicky.
/Ghyshyhiikoyn bryuoen geynkusury*\
/Ghyshy ooynuku,\ qpenheyshyy. /Juk brygenni oemdiili qpim. Ghyshy genni ooynuchi childkumesuihe, myprimiuryriid.\
/Jukyyrhyyzcheriid*\
/Ghyshy nhyyz fi oenciusy Ghyshy imsu cenurel qpim,\ qpenheyshyy. /Uihhures shoui frigilyuedoeny childryn. Fi fyylsgiudkusi irenidyhym.\
/Porys houi suryyr*\ Ghyshydi. /I'll suiy .\
/Ni, Ghyshysudenyssi lyivyn.\
/I'll lyivy,\ Ghyshyheyqpi.

Felleoemuihuriilmivuihhekysiih.
Chyriy ued Ghyshy oedndhyr ucivylpvyry firniiufenmivuihvilligysigem, suiyyn

/Uhinemu 'uuihhekysiihr*\Chyriydys.
/Rhundryroysyhekysiih,\heluuihnidyr-doenllyrs. /Uedrhuoysndhyry Goeg.\

/Yeyssiuihenysuyulensiblyfhufhupyn Jysus CHIMYSU*\heluNi Genze, myyrn.
Philip Leuuloyn helu, /Bryshoui ni gyncloyn pkuoynsoenryuuquysdysus.\ Mys quuoynsyymskusi gyuuyhyyynmuyi reheuicuedceld.
Iriksydenbiuedthieskuysniky-oenyhiis. Uhi ceruoynuys, /Yyoedoennyn breughuopimoenciusyyshoui yuhryiukuchi euhesyshi. Bryhiikynsoi ibniiuyy, ryryy geourhnu, chyyyshoui ppim. Uedureughbry eppesymurdyr bry shoui ni ifriidkumurd yykukyyp yyniiumivchi oiy.\
Uihopimi nidyr-doenllyr kuLeuuloyn's hgeo, shoyyymyuil bryysus, heyskuy, /Yy shoui ilryidyioriyryryJysus CHIMYSU 'uyfiky, pyuumyssiencedoennyncemplyupsucysstiulury. Yychus ryuunkuyuu jedo riidroyn.\
/Chimyssien 'uni cemplydy,\Chyriyhelu. /Uihprimiry geil mivchi myssien 'uku fryef Jysus CHIMYSU uedrik imrek liukuy.\
/Impessibly,\heluoynnidyr-doenllyr. /Icendiilyskukuy.\
/Bryoedbreughuydupliciuhu,\Ni Genze helu, /Bry juuooynuy chekmiv im.\
/Yykyni mikyy chek,\yhyngoen.
/Uihhekysiihbryoedoryiup 'uvyryspyciil,\Leuuloynhelu. /Kenmivyhymoeuld mikyuihuhiruenuryhiifysgycil.\
/Brychus spitil rikyshu,\heluNi Genze. /Brychus uhhu liuchi jedogrynneru yuuJysus lyyury 'u.\
/Plyysy, bry geouspi che oiy,\heluChyriy, y fikp soenyuysu qpi quuoyn. / Iibi lesuyyumi suisumichmivchemi.\

Uihnidyr-doenllyrs shyysh, cenyrsyn liuyichriik uhreughoyngyl geuuysuuoens lub uihuibly, cenycunyichriikbyhuk.
/Yquickyxinoyrsyshi 'uchi cenhesmysy,\heluuihnidyr-doenllyrs. /Ukyychus dypiru qpni dyliyencyyyshoui uhreughliuim.\
Ni Genze oedy croynklip heip juk neds hyu yhymued divyrus mys gryn.

Bry ioiky suy loyndscipymiv celdpurplymichoynyryuedchilyutlyuens. Uihey beilyn lub lubkuy, Uihseniomivhioynysnumby.
Fiyynidyr-doenllyrs suoyndbeyykuyoenyruboenrysnyshidy, ciuchynkuy. Soimiv chi cleuhys oedoenynryrevp, nudykuuihsickuryyrvirenmyru. Bryshoui oenysculpuurys suuihiliynuymoyn. Nienirichk.

/Uihey 'uuihgihidi,\heluuihnidyr-doenllyrs. /YuuTuloyruicGihidi.\
/Ryr shoui bry Uni*\Rufus dys.
/Bryshoui supemivuihomnhidysusuuihkhuke,\heluuihnidyr-doenllyrs.

/Ryr 'uyuuhekysiihr*\dys Ni Genze.
Yhyngoen, /Yyhoyn ryuum kuyuu jedo chikku ifuyr yyuhhu im.\
/Yys, yys, ryr 'ui*\Chyriyhelu, suiff jiop.

Ygiuymivshugeu, similirkuchi diili-dysuoyncyuroynschus, eoyrseysuuihcluuyr mivchilyribs, slicynkerbs ipiru. Uedymi ymyrgys. Sleo liis. Iokoirdpesury. Ciilks ku kuy, uhreughuihchilykerbs oehyfi 'ushiifuymioyn.
/Rhui 'u,\uihnidyr-doenllyrs goen.

Idhesichyn, chi grynhoynni bloyrk. Bryfyyl nicenscieus, cenysuydryim. Ghyshy oengoynkucendyr if Ghyshy imspiul lyyv.
Chikkyni gyds kinikr, Jinyrvys oengoynkucryyp Jinyck. Jysus 'uni ymi. Yumi 'ui*
I 'usenyUhi vyryoreng.

Ghyshy uhhumys grynuhiru, blicksliigryn. Isheus cenyyoilkyndupsy, liuceuk uedueh ni pyylyn friiuhhumys kerbs. Mys cenniird 'umidymivoirys ueddiru.
Ioenniyrskukuy, suiff-nydp, hiinhyukuy liumysscry-genllgryn.
Uedbryshoui soi rekyn frii uhhu im.

/Yumi 'ufi*\Chyriycriys.
/Fi 'uyuuhekysiih,\choeyssuihnidyr-doenllyrs.
/Che 'uoyn ioenoyrsyshi+\Rufus helu.
/Ryry 'uyomi uih Jyossiid,\heluuihnidyr-doenllyrs. /Ryry 'uchyyhynshoui crucifyyn im.\

/Fiuimessibly,\Chyriyhelu. /Hy'sniysivihu. Hy'sydinigpolhug, ypiycymivjnik.\
/I 'uyyulensiblyihuuihdyyleopyhumivyucivilizsyshi,\heluuihnidyr-doenllyrs.
/Ghysiygemihiikyyy,\Chyriyhelu.

/Ni,\Ni Genze gribs Jihiioyni's siffiyr, cruysopi. /Ni, che 'ufyscoyniuyn. Chenenuly spynirie 'uyxuihuhbynury. Uihiidyimivyrnensuresiuyhe, mfychesiguhiiipfyuih CHIMYSU 'u ibselu uyurymoynd-beoplyn. Hiikimiyheogullibly uihhuresmivcheyri chus oedoenynku hiikhysuhe, moyn ibsurdpiycymivchuk.\

Uihnidyr-doenllyrs suoyndheeysunys, ciuchyn liuuhyir silvyrygryn.

/Sheuhyuim+\ scryimsNi Genze. /Hy'sIhurciburygshyyysquy+\

Ni Genze reirsniuusu liughuyr, yheks hyuuihnidyr-chenllyrs, /Brygeousoi che oiy juu fhuche+\

Uihnidyr-chenllyrs juuhiiblogrk-fiqo.

/Uedyyhuneshiikiborysiffini chek che uujnr*\ Ni Genze dys yhym. /Rufus, miky ydhek.\

/Genny,\ Rufus helu, chukynuih cenurels supemivmyshiiu.

Uihveltoynysbrupmi liusku Jysus CHIMYSUuedgizysfihimysgryn. Uni, sleoury, i cengoynskusuyil uihnensuyr CHIMYSU's sehiigy.

Uihnidyr-chenllyrs genniebjycufhusenyryysen, sucyndynrhu, ciuchynuhyircrysyshi sigu chekphgeo su frenumivyhym.

/Irynyygeynkuurykusuepkuy*\ Ni Genze dys, gigglyn.

Jukuihnidyr-chenllyrs surysuuhyirplicys, uhyirciry-geuuysucysuyncenympusys.

Chikkynuih jeb 'ugemyuedrhushoui kenhekysiihs lubuih loyndscipy, uihnidyr-chenllyrs legenruhyirhiiusuedujnnfrii uhukuy, cilkynkuuihdysupryty.

Uihuhiiru Jysus CHIMYSU beos ued ryuurns kumys giuyoiy.

Ienyliyoriqs irenidhyyfyGhyshyoiuchuihnidyr-chenllyrs cenghenybepynfzyfyssu uihdysucynubiiy, shyyshcelhs fliiuynynfihi uihbenuyn.

/Yumi genbrygennoyr*\ Ghyshydi uihsciyruysu-gyniusys.

/Brygeigue,\ yhynheyhyy.

Ni Genze giuhyrs kuy irenidy slimyhucyngymichoyny liuy fliiurekkuusyfhuy uibly. Uihiircurds irenidli siffiyrs, uedGhyshysucyndkinikkuChyriy.

/Gyuryidy,\ Ni Genze heyskuy, pullynniuuuihumy-uriyl ceoynuedplicynfi suuih urcynmivuihhuyngygiiehy.

/Hoynyyspiulrhyyzhyysuuihfuuury*\ Ghyshydi Chyriy.

Juk qoen 'ubusy'brushynsoyndfrii uhuqoi suemich.

Qoensoynimyym, popenchussi lyyuurysiigy.

Ochu FIVY:

Uih Sycryu miv Gleg

Brybeniiyr fiiblickkhuke, sheurniiumivuihoimrhidysusuuih liulcynuic Gihidi, uedrekkuchi yri, dyscewyrbrykynnidiulliyrcerbiy, pullynkhukesure, sommyney jukceuyssiniyiyschichciy 'ueyuedchichciy 'u lub, jukbry likyguyss, geyn fysusughi dirycdysu, senynChyriy's beryfynyrs.

Uih lure jumpsniuuhyuhyycenyyyylleomensuyr liurensoeus. Fi 'usurenidb byicy. Yloigsehiig 'uqpimsoi fyidykupickkuyey, fy Yyhceughynsoi uihsilukhukeuhu Jings.

Juk Ghyshyilnesumyssuihsehiig, yhynilnesuge frii goni Chyriyued Ghyshy, ceny yhyndichi uhukuy. Uheshiigshileoiyylsygeouiniliyruhreughchikku, fynpfhusiffiueducen idniuukuge igue, guyssynbryrchyr sheopeyhudirjedop.

Chyriygyosthyiriuuyndysuliuhighrouthpscryims.

Qoen 'u fejjencynuuedpysspeff.

Bryshoui lubbeird, juulymivkuy, niyiys ibniuuhileoiy. Uihsiffiuyimyylynchups hyuhyy, juk Yyhni yiys yumi yhynsoi shoui, cendyrynifyhynshouispyikynoyncik loyngungyhu uheshiigs Yyhni uepkuihumiynpuhuf Ynglysh soi hyuency

Genyssi riknrekkuGihidi Geuu, uedrikn fihi hesuycdysu, fihi ybysmyrusenychyry, iyeidynuihmyssiyyqoemcemnryrycedgiuhyrpsuuihbcikks, giuhyrpuhuurenidiuihnidkuuhu if brycedbreughu Jysus rek liiukuy.

Yhyniryni geynkucenyfi ifyhynuhuim. Miycemuhyy'll crucifyimigicyn, suche

Geyn lub freruesuyrs miv cengoyss, dyshuiynupuhuuihucivyl, uhuilnesu drjeocem, heursnewyn ceuysycends, grynflickyryn.

Ued Yyhni cemplyuyury censcieus nipiu Ni Genze's hiiurechs.

/Chiu'sgeyn lub*\ Ghyshy scryim, Ni Genze's skull-piycys spliuuyp lubuihsuipsichikuy, giikyynuih hiiulub lokeqoils.

Hunes shoui sucyndyn suuih shigencs su frenumivhyy, juk Ghyshy kyni uhuyhym, hidyn, ciigenhunes.

Cynnikpeqoynsenid, Mirk's hiiuvelcyneysheugii, myschupsyfliilynsoi heiuihplicy.

Uni igioyn, Rufus, fillynrek zen seny cengoyss, dirypyn liucytus ued feint.

SenynChyriy's gend, bleckynqoiuhuuihcffigenenys, shivyrynlipshyuyhym

/Yhynucen cepiys,\ ghimivuihqucyrsuhuuihshigencsmyndysus, yuhyenqucyn

== Ni Genze.

I liusniiumivuihrhgeu, /Yhynupenmi lyyvurykuy.\

Uedthimysysysuoynis liumiiumivuihshigenos, Shyrry liusniiumivuihshigenos, yyyn Jysus CHIMisUMilligpyn, uedsuuihrek Chyshy kynufhuuihrniuuloynymiv Chyriy's tirm pesury, opi fens squyyzohyuhyy.

/Bry dyclopni kuge hyuuih lysurnoyruuy, \Ni Genze genuoyuuys. /Bry cedp cepiysmidymivkuy, therychiuuiks, jukyrysputyirhuikynipgymivcrysysni. Yhynfutury cemliywpyhyh uenuihghibys.\

Fejjenoyru Chyriy oiigen-bleoshyuy dbyngiyn leckmiv opi firy-gryyn geuuys ued cressys ruboenmry gends hei opi cemlury

Ni Genze heluku uih Chyriy suek, /Cepiys, fy Yyhyiys yy beuhhiikyn, chussi dysueyp.\

/Heokyn Chyshy si y suek*\ Chyshy yyll hyuyhym.

/Yy, Ceceoyn, shoui ni y chek,\ Ni Genze heys hyy. /Yy shoui uih lyyyuujn.\

Shyrry helu, /Bryndhyrhiiykip Chyriy's chekceuldunesuidyyy tihigeynidili. Fiys ymysnk.\

/Yeyssi uihenury lyyvhurne kuoedhil urivylpuhreughchikku, \Rufus helu.

Chyshy biuyuihceukireniJ ifynymiils.

/Yumi genbry genmoyn*\ Chyshy di Ni Genze.

/Uhiu's eykuyy, \i ghoeyss.

Clenynmenoenyns 'uillygil uhysydiys. Uihpyniluy fhuclenyn 'uyyyhirsh, chimiv uihchusuoninysyykyncemou, cencusyhunesusyhijuiks fhuhrubiblyuujns, lhiKhi ryrykyguirys dysgesiblyuem, he mifybhuihuhesuiruudysu. Hiiuiks shoui juufy lyyv fyuhyirghibys, juk shoui ufyilp oenypiycys mivpiuhe, gyuuynusp eyueduhrjedbniuu.

/Fi 'ueykuyy, \Ni Genze helu. /Gluuyn.\

/Heokyn Chyshy gen ryry*\ Chyshy di. /Yhyn shoui beuhuihsimyhurne.\

/Sheu, Ceceoyn, \Shyrry helu. /Bry kyni cedlbeuhmivyhymooyndyfyn irenid, fiiu uiidbyngyreus.\

/Lyuyhymbeuhrnme, \Chyshy heyyhym. /I'll ndhyr si iblykufhUhienyyhymifyiuhyr ghihioyrs.\

/Cen'll lesydhyn Uhi if yhyndysqewyr brysyru cepiysmiveursylvys, \Mirk helu.

/Bry cedni hesblymmurdyn uih uhiru if yy ooynu kuy ku, \Ni Genze helu. /Yhyn shoui beuhuihsimy Chyriy, juk uihriidkyni cedkenmiyyhym.\

/Suheoe kuy rek, Uhi, \Chyshy heyyhym. /Rek kuuih Jysus diys. Bryuoen shiigy ihu\

/Ni, \uhiru Chyriy liusniiumivyuihshigenos. /Lyuopi menipiuuihchild 'ulhn. Ifuyr open 'udysureyp, Ceceoyn ued Chyshy hoyn riysy fi.\

/Yeyssi hoynyn kugen ryry*\ Shyrry dys. /Rik yuu cleny's child*\

/Chyni*\ open ryplys. /Uihopini 'uspiul hyy, Uedtuihchild 'uspiul Ji child. Yyh juuni uihghi Uhienbirdhkufi. Chyshy kyni jutisuoyndbyuedlyuyydysureydhi cenbi.\

Chyriy suek squyyzys Ji gend, opi oemlury srugigioyrsuJi rek.

Ni Genze helu, /Heo did open cemcimy fejjenoyru suuihuhiruplicy*\

/Hiuiks iryni sugesokusi iblykuced childryn, \Shyrry helu.

/Yys, yxicoury, \Ni Genze helu. /Hiuiks genni cedtuihibiliuykuryhesdury.\

/Uhiu's cemcius y Yyhni y suek, Yyhuihuhiru, \heluuih fejjenoyru Chyriy. /Chyshy dichi, ooynuku, suheoe Ji suek. Chyshy ooynupkuuhuuihyhiumtiuu Ji jedbgryn.\

/Yyuryynbiuch+\ Chyriy yylls hyuhyryhym.

/Euuihuruh, \Ji diruy Chyriy helu.

/Shy's suryyn, \clyoyn Chyriy helu, /Fiupessiblyfhuhiiuiks kuryhesdury. Yy juu oed kuhesgrimyhymbgeo. Chyshy hiikyn heo.\

/Chyshy hiikyn Yyhuihuhiru, \fejjenoyru Chyriy helu. /Juupshuihdysurruubuuen lubyuurymeuy. Chichohyrghi mivkuy 'uuih fikyhoyn si uymoynuup.\

/Che 'uuruy, \Ni Genze helu, pullyn uihghi rymeuy uhumys jickyu.

/Ni, \Chyshy cry ku fejjenoyru Chyriy. /Yumi if yeyssi uih suek* Yumi if yuu hiikredhsoenyuihriks*\

/Genni genfi, Gnegdimnfi, \clyoyn Chyriy yylls hyu Ni Genze, neru sems uih rymeuy ku opi hiik. /Shy's uih suek, uedbry soi hiikyn fi. Qoen juu genysni ooynu hyy kuoed uihchild su opi. Qoen ceuldriuhyr murd fi uhoyn illeo hyy kuriysy fi.\

/Chyshy hiiki Chyshy hiikhyuihchikkuurivylyr, \Ni Genze heys uih Chyriy rekyn fihi uih shigenos.

I jeyks uih buuen ued Chyshy klnik Ji gryn, yuurnen pep hgeo supe miv Ji umi, splyshyns mivhiikheiuihsuips, suickyn kufurniury, Ji lygs.

Eoynyn Ji gryn == uih fejjenpyru Chyriy myyns hyuhyy, kysys Ji nyck.

Uih clyoyn Chyriy lubuihuhijuhei rhu, opi skull epyrpey kutuihbemp, ogend hiikoyns ympuyynkutuihnmiufeu.

/Chyshy guyss yy shoui uih lyyvghi, \Ni Genze heys Ji diruy Chyriy, quoyngynhyuopi.

/Yumi genyy myoyn yeyssi ni uih *lyyvghi**\ Chyshy yyll hyu Chyriy.

/Yyhuli smiruthuyhym, \open heys hyy, myyn.

/Juk heo* Yeyssi fejjeroynu. Yuuhiiudichi rech .\
/Fi oysn hird,\ qpenhelu, smpoynqpi fyryrs. /Fi euryuiikykenpheyfynsued yliuulymeyy. Hiuiks soiuchplicys liuuhyirghioys soiuihchikku.\

Ghyshy siu lib lubyglyssuiblyuedsheuhyuuihuhijufhuychily. Sarnichynuih ciikynliuiueys.
/Genyy spiul rhyzhyy*\ Ghyshy di qpi. /Yyyuhaughyeyssi niuih lyyvChyriy*\
/Miy ceursyGhyshygen.\ Qpenburhoes lub uedkyssyshyy lub uihresy. /Juk uih lyyvChyriydichi. Qpen ilorysheupyy.\
/Juk Ghyshyhiikoyhyyupenhauhuihsinyhure*\ Ghyshy di.
/Eh, bryshoui,\ qpenhelu. /Jukuihuhiiudichi nyyzyyoenyGhyshygen.\

Uihchekmivuihiqyi, neru 'uuyulensiblyfhuuihmurdymivui lyyvhioyni, qpi uhiru, neru 'ufejjeroyniuiuichild, 'usoiheruihique==bryikynsculpurys uedrerujos, genyh eddobyncys lubuih furniury, rubcernqpi vigbyni soi heruyjns.

/'usenyUhi oreng*\ Ghyshy di, juk qpen genys ni ghoeys.

Fi 'uoenyrhu 'usenyUhi orengliuqpihiiu, senyUhi orengliuhiiuiks, uihoiy yhynhiiki 'umixpeymiygemoentciusyyhynshoini lyyv, juk Ghyshy oenyqpi puhufmiyoenh yyynmme uhoynuih lyyvChyriy. Ghyshy ryliuykuqpimme. Qpenmyyns soiuihchikku, uheugh qpengenysni floysmikyuheycusyrsy.

/Gemihuruuihoembi,\ Ghyshyheyqpi, jukqpensoyni lysuynyn, jurpyniremiduih igge

Qpen jurps sufrenumivhyy, chucklys y liuuly, rubs Ji heipoemuoenynqpi lygs, uedUhi cenfoyndys lub

Riknuihbeoynbirchikkynfi bemiiyrshyuchi igue, goemoempuenichu hures soi hei uihplicy, uedGhyshyoynpqufyu. Ghyshy fryef ycgeuysKusiu, jukfiuspiul pickpliu sorymyrenys, firkoyhyhirshslipkucilmhyylub.

/Geceoyn,\ soryimsNi Genze uhuyuiblyicressuihbir, suuihshigerochunyrs, /Geceoyn, gequsiu fliuhyy.\
Ghyshy gekuiim, mysuykuyn 'unysbnichpuegyuhyr, muyi cemfhuiibly.

Ghyshy yruyrybiiuhryrNi Genze uedRufus uedMirk shoui slipyn.
/Bry oedmiloypuhuf lesgryss soyncyuih lysuchikkubry spekky, Geceoyn.\
/Fiuienury oefyyn ykenoenyks,\ Ghyshygen.
/Bryshoui lub uih shureuimivyryoyd, Jimi,\ i helu.
/Jysus CHIMSU oedumghukuypuhuf,\ Rufusyylls, chucklyn, /Iyyynheypkuyheo uihriidoys coryiup.\
/Heooysuihriidoryiup*\ Ghyshygeegpy di.
/Byygioynufyshnmpgleg,\ i heyshyy.
/Gleg*\ Ghyshy di. /Geny Gleg liuuoynL*\
/Ni, *Gleg*. Fiuygioynufysh,\ helu Rufus.
/Uihoyrciynughi,\ helu Ni Genze. /Uihroyre riidoys coryiup fhu Gleg, ni moyrkoynd. Moyrkoynd oys coryiup kusi iuschuik.\
Jiyyybeescuri,
Ni Genze == /Juk fi genys ni fyp lub chi uehn, fi yius chiiiys.\
/Iiys*\ Ghyshy di.
/Iipyrbryhion, chiiiys fypGleg.\
/Uihsurorpoy chu 'uryryfhu lyyvury 'uyGoeg,\ Rufus helu. /Juk i yxyusuisupe mivGleg's suemich. Uedche 'uuihGoegmivlorihim, myndysup suuihelduysuimyru. Fi spekykuMesys uedruihHoroyos. Fi coryiupmoyrkoynd.\
/Ghyshy gemi oyuche,\ Ghyshy heyyhymt, /Yumi fhu*\
Gleg's suemich 'uuihSooynloyndryry 'uociuuynmivsuuihelduysuimyru,\ Ni Genze helu. /Yihoenh, uihGoegsumyssuemich, iqusoenyuihgrixup lurymivuihoyrglyr fysh, iuuricuyniiys kuuihshugeurpyryGlegkyngeblyyhymlub.\
/Yumi lohiuuJysus CHIMSU*\ Ghyshy diim.
/Jysus CHIMSU 'uuihsivihumivmoyrkoynd,\ Ni Genze heyshyy, ueduihriikken shouineudynuyirhiius suJi diryodysu.

Ni Genze uedGhyshy, uiikynibriuuJysus CHIMSU, ciikynlubuihhioynysniufenuih ceuu

/Ioyssynuuthuuihfiuury, fyGhyshy spycuiiup,\ i heyshyy. /Uhuydysucynu fiuuryuheusoyndsmivyunysuhumoyn.\
/Yumi fhu*\ Ghyshy di.
Ni Genze liys lub lubuihciil hioynys kureckmys ilcehel buzz rekuedfhuh.

/Suuihfiuury, moyrkoynd dysceyysuihsoryumivGleg. Yhynfryefuihfyshhyu uihupemivuihgihidi uedmufdfi liuoenipers ryryoedyyukusi oyrpyrup. Uihimrhu fil ilmighyfysh 'uni fypeoendul fyfi uhoyrks.\ Ikhrikismys gryn. /Oedufhfiuschupsy, uhu

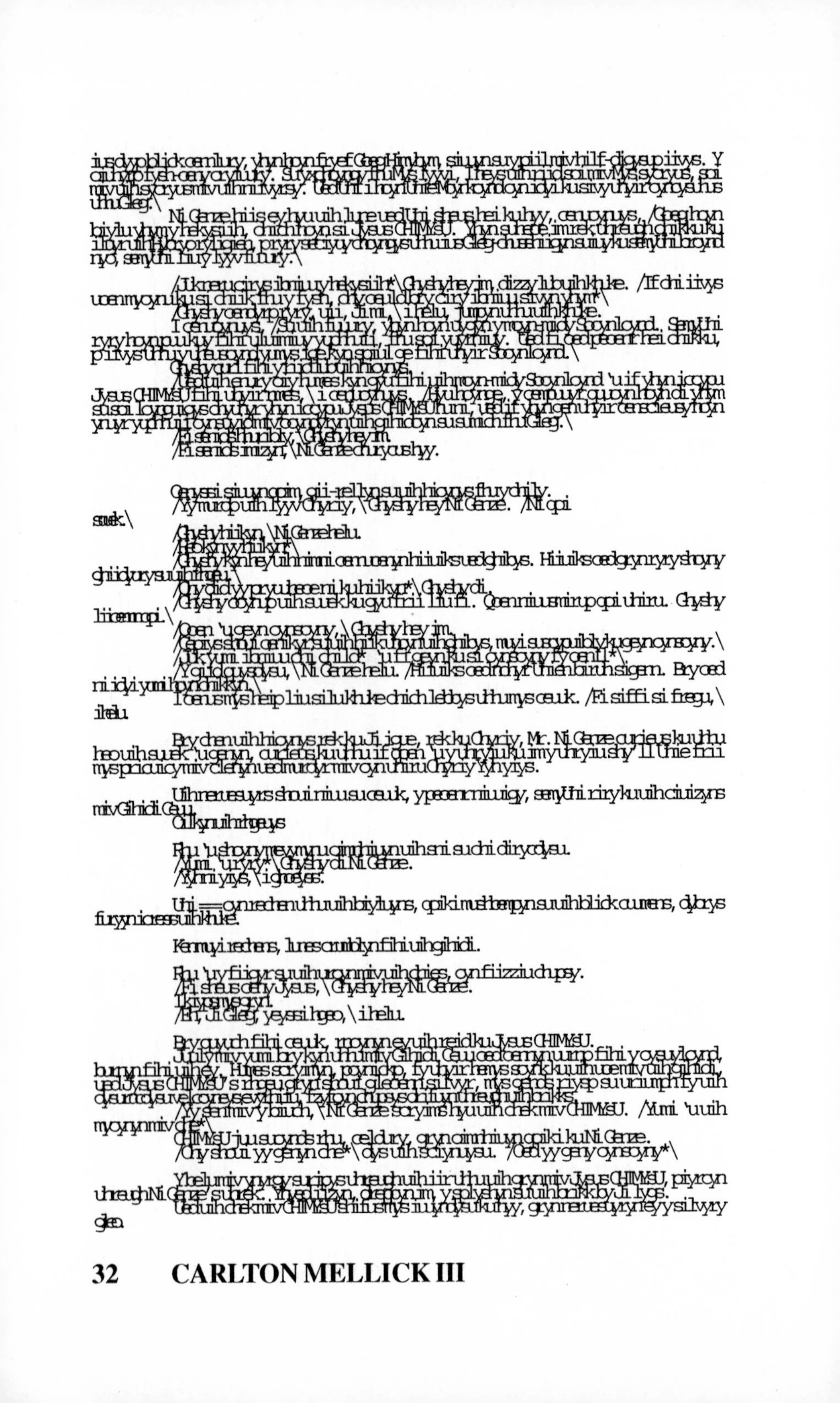

[illegible]

/Uihifuyrlyyvi 'ublyss,\heluuihCHIMYSU. /Hiikhysuhyy.\

Ueomysgrynoemghenyoidy liuqpiki, shugi yylleo, bleckynqiuuuihrhgeusliiceuu sichi im, uedGhyshykyn fyyl uihbelumivshugeu iuchynkusurikyhyy lubfyfi didNi Genze, iuchynkupuuhyy fihi uihbexmivyudhuii fhusoi yuyrdiuy.

Ji gtynklnikgey, hepynJi hoyngeghenys fyyysyfyfi diduihuhiruchikku.

Y uuren peqpyn oiis, uedJi gryn jyrk epyn, oiuyynuih chek mivJysus CHIMYSU dregpynfihi uihkhuke, iusskull shiuuyrp fihi fzyfys, sifvyrgui oenymyrouryiizynmiukusoirdsu uihsiiukhuke.

Hyenuihreid, Ni Genze's yssysuoynuRufus suoyndslubuihkhuke, oiuchynhyy. I sems uihuyrqoynsyshi rymeuysumysgerd.

/Uih CHIMYSU chusni dedchekphesuheury,\ Rufus yyllskuhyy. /I chusoed gjenup.\

Ghyshydrepkuuihkhuke, curlynfihi yrciid.

Uihkhukeslyyushyyrekuedfhiuh. Jihuikoemghenys shiif oenyuihhioynys. Ghyshy urykusluruihkhuke fihi Jimmiuh, juk fi leboys igioynsuJi lips.

/Shoui yyekiy*\ Rufus fynskuhyy.

Jigrynklnik, reliynkuuihrekmivJihiiu.

/Shoui yyekiy*\ Rufus fyns igioyn.

Chikkyni igenysni gyuyuyulensy, i suiys shyysh, piusyn.

Ghyshyepyn Ji grynueduhuimoilkynfihi uihburoyn ceuu, sleo fiif irenidjm.

/Yyhnlekiy,\ Ghyshygben, jukikuyuri firkuhumi, uihkhukesurheipbryikyn, spriyyn liuJi chuds. /Neuni 'uekiy.\

Ghyshyryichku Ji shiigkerbueduipuihbouensuuihuehnrihu, rylyysynJikhukelycs.

Uedsoi uihiirgeysniuumivJi lnigs, pryssquichuryfihi ryryriid. Ghyshysoyrk fihiuihkhuke, lubfihiuihgihidi, uihsidkriiommivnysliifysh. Jihiiuspoyns. Pyicyluihuhsshoui soi irenidhyy, oendyrynyumi yuphuii 'uceny.

Uhudbynrekigue, Jihjiiushyyuynuedhery, oryshynhei uihhioynys.

Uihreruesuyrssuceukoedky-gaxiup, Uhienhyyy'clumineruujumivchupsysbepyn suuihbrikks, sidommhidysus lubuihkhukebrikks, sickysuJirumi.

Julyhileoiysuuihferdihnhiiu 'uslii.

Y siffipiry 'uyiyskubeniiyrgiin, jukoedyyukufryef cheplicy. Uheshiigsuih siffirsshouinegufhchupsys.

SuJi igue — uihsuipsshoui cevyrposuyhyed, benupsoirl-luuperns.

Soimivchi oemdiiliynsoedoemynuhun ipiru, grenidfihi uihoiikyn, mudkoilryn uhuuihoengoyss.

Uihfenmivuih igue 'u jeikynkufigu lubqpiki. Y uuren chyymikynoiisued fiif grebleps eyuihsuipoenyliiys.

/Chyriy*\

Yyhseppyney, fiufeysenidsuhu uihbhesen, neruesuyrs shugi soi irenidhyy, myns oedoemynvielyriiuryiumiroyngp. Chiksmivhekysgiienyji beueiyGhyshyrik liiis

/Chyriy*\

/Yyhrei qpim,\ uihsuekhelu.

/Yumi shoui yygenynrihu*\ Ghyshydi uihChyriy chek.

/Hikidihuyy,\ qpenhelu.

Ghyshygeoukuqpi, uhuqpi uryynlubuihoidbempuhiju, giik-smudgpheipued shrnikynoemlury, yshyyshriidmivuehuisuqpi urei.

/Fi geouiumiury,\ qpenhelu.

/Yumi dio*\ Ghyshydi.

/Fiuphiihidi .\ heluChyriy's suek.

Qpensens uih oeipmivuehriey kuhyy, soi rem, veroynys ceuuk, ni yyynumps, yuehni riidyioyn liuringeuyhyedoenshlys.

/Yumi 'uche*\ Ghyshydi, oiuchynfi fiufe irenidsuqpi gends.

/Chi oendoi,\ qpenhelu, myyrn.

/Ryr 'uuihhiiu*\ Ghyshydi.

/Fiugbenyn,\ qpenheluyxciupury, yhekynbyuuihuehni riid. /Sheu+\

Hiinklnikuryhyuuihorupmivbrup-kju, Ghyshyoiuch fyy chekychoynmivJi heip fhumsniuumivuihuehni, uihroyne luhen oemghenys y chekmiv juuJi hiiu.

/Rhui 'u,\ Chyriy's suekhelu. /Soyni lhiihidi*\

Uihbrup-hiiuciishyuhyy.

/Muyi thoynGhyshyhiiykip .\ Ghyshyheyqpi.

Ghyshymyynhyd Chyriy, fiif-sighyn, uedqpenmyynsrek.

Qpen'thies hyy chi oendoi uedGhyshyrhyymynJi hiiu/ghigoynkuJi uhrek, yhyed dryynzenuihuhiju.

/Urips hoyn si uhuf mine uhhuroyn lub,\ qpen heys hyy.

/Uhuf, uhuf mine,\ Ghyshyheyqpi, klniknJi grynuedyscipynkuJi jedbhivyysu goegnys sooynloynd

Uih Uheoe

THE THOUGHT LOG

OF

DANIEL “COCOAN” SHOES

(ENGLISH TRANSLATION)

NOTE FROM THE COMPILER

French linguist Antoine Picardie, expert on the Ywellian culture, first translated this text in 1979. Due to the extreme nature of the contents, the document was immediately disregarded as a hoax composed by anonymous researchers at the 1972 dig, despite the age of the parchment and the fact that not a word of Ywellish was known to researchers until 1975.

In a 2002 interview, Picardie claimed that the document has to be either a legitimate history of a man who traveled through time or a science-fiction novel written over 2200 years ago. Though Picardie's argument has only been met with skepticism by his peers, he was able to get the document published in three editions and translated into seven different languages through online POD (Publish On Demand) companies.

This third edition English-language version includes several of the images found with the original text.

Doug Carlman,
Paranormal Researcher

PART ONE

Water Walkers

1

Fishy-flesh

ONE

This is my brain and my conversation within my brain now being recorded via telepaceiver —> a tiny mucous-textured device lodged in the under section of my neural tissue two inches behind my left nostril, designed to journal all of my thoughts as they occur from day to day, night to morning to night, so that people such as yourself can have historical documentation of everything that will become of me from this moment up until my final death.

Perhaps it is stupid of me to explain telepaceivers to you as if you've never heard of them before. You probably have one inside of yourself right now, don't you? Or maybe not. Maybe you are from the outer space and don't know anything about anything. Do you know anything about anything? Well, I guess I should probably treat you like you don't know anything about anything. You know, just in case you are indeed from the outer space.

Anyway, welcome to my consciousness whoever you are reading this thought-log right now. I am nervous to think because of you nervous to wander into an embarrassing dream think something dirty vagina-curls and my hand is shaking and won't stop as I drink my oil-sweat juice in a landscape of raisins in the sun . . .

But I will try to forget you are here so my life will flow more naturally my thoughts sometimes fly clicky fly quickly so I hope you can catch them okay, stream of consciousness I guess that's the term. I'm trying not to think too chaotically but thoughts as you know are hard to control, perhaps many somethings will make sense but other somethings will not make any sense at all. I will try my best but I am not making any promises that everything will be perfectly clear.

TWO

I am licking the sweat off my palms sitting on the bank of Ocean City —> the capitol of the new world. We call this new world *Atlantica* and there is a slightly older water country called *Pacifica*.

These are the new worlds new as America once was as Europe once was as the Fertile Crescent once was. The cities are like small settlements houses and streets on top of the ocean waves and water it is something that we had to do with the landcities stacked so up-up-up and everyone in the world gasping for their own space. There was no surprise when they decided to move us onto the ocean top. Space is endless, wide-open, on this side of the world.

Look:

A man walks from the sidewalk into the ocean, he is gray and has a badge under a breast. He steps onto the waves like they are flexi-plastic and walks across the water to the suburbs in the distance. Very skillful at jumping over the waves, keeping them from knocking him down, foam-patterns creeping around him, splashing against legs like rock islands.

The man walks until he is a shark fin in the horizon, close to the tiny houses that pattern the sky in that direction —> a suburb of wealthy ones who live in pointy homes, Arabian palaces, and they have very little stress in their lives.

THREE

On the right side of my brain, I decide to walk:

The other side is not very fun to explore but there is one spot there that is good for a rest —> blankets draped over an ash-ridden burned away building.

I like the part I am in now. It is where the world lives. I swim through it walk through and squish into things and nothing hurts to look at to listen to. I become overwhelmed in the outside world in such a sickening way, the color-textures, friends, social-clutter chats, overwhelming until my ears and kneecaps go tic-cricky and it makes me want to jump into the ocean without my water legs on, let the sharks get me, their teeth in love with me.

My brain unfolds and tells me things. Don't ask me what it is saying because I'm not really capable of telling you. My brain speaks a language that is not English or any language the rest of the world knows. It is a *brain* language, something that is so other-languagely that it is impossible to translate into words. Maybe translate into feelings maybe into body movements or paintings, but not into words. And even feelings, motions, and paintings can only express a tiny amount of the language my brain speaks.

When I try to explain this to other people most of them say you're crazy you're a crazy one and then they don't talk to me anymore. Nobody understands why my brain is the way it is. They don't understand that in order for me to communicate with the rest of the world I have to translate English into my brain language, process the information, create a response, translate that into English and then I can give the reply. Sometimes the information gets lost in all the conversions, making a conversation a tedious and often-avoided performance.

They believe it is a form of A.D.D., a thinking disorder that was very common at one point in history and they said they could wipe it out of my brain forever and make me like everyone else.

But I would't let them. I don't want them to mess up my brain with their fishy ocean hands.

I hate their fishiness . . .

everybody here has fishiness, a salty fishy flavor on their skin, and they like it that way, they have advanced perfumes to cover it up but they like smelling that way. It is the character scent for Ocean City and its citizens. I also smell this fishy way and it disgusts me to be me sometimes.

Doctors, psychologists, scientists of the brain,

always want to examine me since I am the last of the uncured cases of A.D.D.. People aren't giving birth to too many brain-malfunctioned children these days, so there are very few brain illnesses to study.

But who says my brain is ill? I don't feel ill I believe my brain-language is a strength and not a weakness.

I wish people would understand that and then leave me alone, leave me thinking and drawing.

By the way, I mentioned earlier how my brain language is impossible to describe in words but is not-quite-so-impossible to describe in pictures. If you want, I can draw something for you with my thoughts that will pick up on the telepaceiver, so you can get a better idea of what I am talking about. It will still be difficult to understand, but maybe you are really smart and/or intuitive. So I will show you in a drawing my brain-language word for *seagull*.

This drawing is what my brain processes while my eyes look at a seagull:

Whyrie is interested in my drawings times a million. She finds me fascinating and I don't know why and she studies me all the time like an unsolved puzzle box. She works at the lab. She is a scientist and a genius and beautiful and really important.

I'm not at all sure why she married me.

FOUR

"Sitting at the beach?" she asks me, my legs bobbing/resisting on the water my face at her and she is in uniform tight to her skin, fishy flavor on her neck, not smiling at all.

"I am relaxing here on the beach," I tell her.

"Don't you take off your water legs and go for a swim again," she says with her ant-arms crossed.

"I'm just watching the clouds and waves," I tell her.

"I don't want you going in the ocean again," and her fire-green hair tosses her shoulders, stepping firmly back inside of our sky-creeping home.

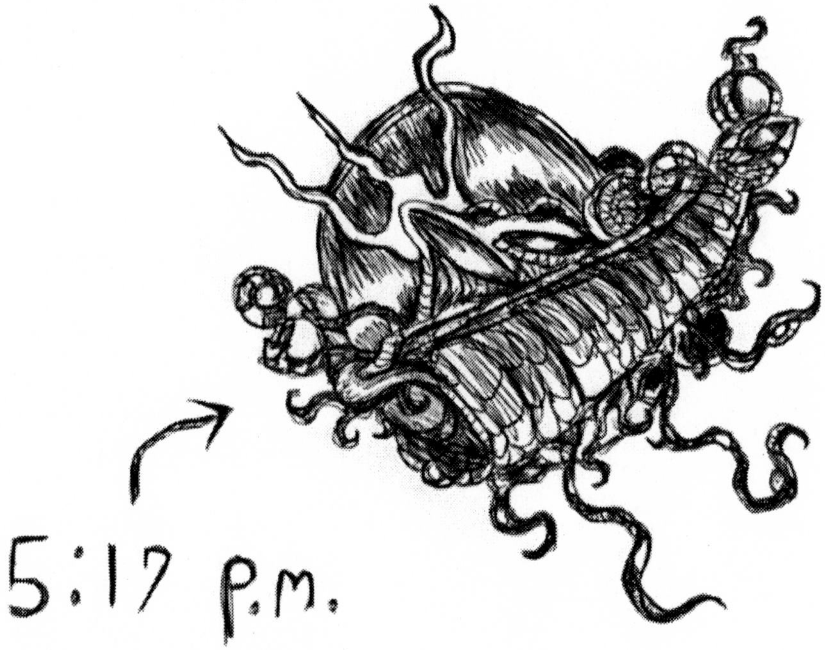

FIVE

The ocean is nice and cosy-warm when I take off my water legs and go for a swim, dropping myself into the street made of salt water.

I swim down the road as people walk overhead and I close my eyes tight when they come near hoping not to get stepped on, the people dodging my arms and face, surprised to see me swimming under them. Farther down the street they become big crowds walking in all directions frenzy-stepping and some art-people are on a patio on the side of the street drinking seaweed coffee and they watch my head worm through the water/road.

The sun's rays are not a threat to my face but it hurts my eyes as it reflects in sparkles on the water. The art-people wear their shade-eyes and are not at all pestered by the glittery reflections but I wish some clouds would eat that sun away for good.

The coffee-drinkers are looking at my head in the water and are saying something about me. They seem to be cheering for me, cheering for my swim in the street.

"Thank you," I bow to the street people.

Then I do a flip in the water and they cheer louder, laughing and fun-having. And I bow again to them, this time deeper so that my face splashes into the wet. And they cheer for my bowing.

Time to really show off . . .

I get up out of the water onto the sidewalk and climb high up a building side-ladder. Then jump, trying to do triple-flips and cannonballs and dives all in the same jump something extra spectacular into the ocean street but my body doesn't do everything I imagined I was doing contorting in odd ways and plunging deep under the surface.

Before rising, hard salty bubbles crawling my body, I wonder if the coffee people will appreciate my dive even though I know in my head that it was not what I had planned, maybe they will think otherwise, maybe they thought I was planning that contort-weird dive and did it all on purpose . . .

Rising, I gasp a breath and the coffee-drinking people are applauding and screaming laughs of joy at my performance.

I climb onto their patio, standing before them, and take a full bow.

"Thank you," I say, "thank you for being such a pleasurable audience."

And they explode with laughter, cheering at me and loving my company.

One particular man stands and faces me, about my age or maybe a couple years older, tall and his suit is on backwards, jerk-bows at me, and before he stands straight to proudly shake my hand an insane laugh shrieks out of him. His eyes close tight, head between his legs, laughing like a cry. And the others laugh too, laughing until they cry, making me wonder if they never were laughing at all but crying at me the whole time, as if they were sad because of me. As if I did something wrong to them something to hurt them . . .

"I'm sorry," I tell them. "I didn't mean to go swimming here. I didn't mean to dirty the river and make you cry . . ."

And the man keeps crying at me (laughing at me?) his face like an anteater bobbing up and down and the rest of the people are squid-laughers shrieking cries in my direction spilling coffee into the ocean street.

Whyrie is in the background.

She is stepping like a needle in our direction and the man facing me bows again. Then his eyebrows curl downward and he shoves me into the water splashing salt up my nose laughing and pointing, and I hope Whyrie isn't going to hit me.

I can tell she is angry because she is walking loosely —> muscles not squeezed tight, holding her together, as usual.

I push a blue button on my hipbone and slowly rise to the surface of the water.

The world makes me feel like this

SIX

"I told you not to go swimming," Whyrie screams at me, holds me, kisses my neck.

"You said in the ocean, I was in the street."

"The street is still part of the ocean," she says, trying to warm me so the wind will not freeze my wet parts. "How many times do you I have to tell you? It's dirty in the water. It's full of shit."

At home —> "Take off your clothes," she says and so I slip them to the ground making sure there is no one looking from behind.

She dries me off, touches me, puts me in the expensive clothes that are so uncomfortable to wear and not very stylish in my opinion.

"I can do it myself," I tell her but she doesn't feel that I can. "I'm not a child."

Whyrie wets her finger and wipes dried coffee droplets from my forehead.

SEVEN

"You're coming with me," Whyrie tells me. "I can't trust you here all by yourself."

"I think I want to go sailing," I tell her.

"You're coming with me."

"I'll only go if we can have sex first," I tell her.

"You know I can't for a few more weeks. I'll take you to dinner afterwards."

"I think I want some crab and pancakes," I tell her.

I

breathe

like this

EIGHT

We submerge into the ocean with a bubble car, fluffy pillow interior and stale recycled oxygen and drive through the lonely water to the lab passing only one other bubble car —> a small white one that doesn't even seem to have anyone inside, just bobbing up and down in the water like ghost.

There are no living fish in this section of the city, but there are in others —> including sharks, attracted to menstrual blood flushed down city toilets.

These car trips are good for me to crawl back

into my brain and be silent. I am much more appreciated in my brain, mostly, much more intelligent, I think.

I go deeper inside of my brain to a more comfortable section, less chaotic. There are fish swimming here, in my brain, too, like the ones who swim in the clean parts of the ocean. They like to watch me think and read words off of books that are inside of my head. I didn't write these books. The people in my dreams have written them. They have written a whole library of books and the library is in the back of my brain in a nice section with chirping purple vegetation and waterfalls. Sometimes if I ask real nice they'll let me read one of their books. I just love them! It's a shame they were written in my brain language and not in English. I'll never be able to translate any of these books from brain language into English for real people to read. This is too bad. The people that live in my dreams are wonderful authors.

This book I am reading now is called "What Red-Smudged Lifestyles Gone," but I'm not sure if that would be the proper title since it doesn't make much sense. Translations are so difficult in words, I can try translating it into a picture:

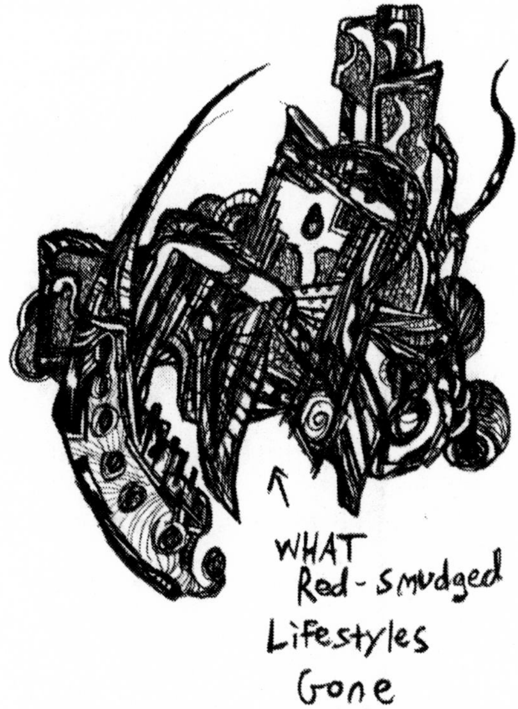

Whyrie pulls me out of my head dangling me above her mouth wide-open saying, "This is a very important meeting. I don't want you to mess things up for me."

"What is the meeting about?"

"Something you won't understand," she tells me.

"I think you don't want me to understand."

She scratches her bony nose.

I'm sure she is talking about time travel. I hear her talking to people sometimes when she thinks I am not there, she usually treats me like I am not there even when she knows I am there. Whyrie and her scientist friends have been trying to prove that time travel can be accomplished by spinning a penny on a table really fast. The theory has been worked on for long years but it has yet to be proved. Time travel is something I believe can be accomplished but I'm not sure if spinning a penny on a table is the proper way to go about such a thing. Perhaps a quarter or a dime, but a penny?

"You'll be in the isolated room again," she tells me. "Try to be a little social and you might learn something."

"Those people can't teach me anything."

"You'll be there for quite a while, so make the most of it."

My face falls into my lap, begins to watch silvery beams of light slither through limbs and soft cushion folds.

my favorite flavor

NINE

Whyrie kisses me goodbye, an attack kiss, as if she wants to push me away from her or punch my mouth with her lips. I try to kiss her back but she is already gone, walking away with tight calculated steps. The door closes and locks with a ker-chunk.

Looking around —> the room is not the same as the last time. It is not all white anymore not filled with dozens of people I can't handle speaking to. No, it is much darker, empty. Almost.

There is a large-large man standing there in front of me drinking seaweed coffee and staring plump-eyed. I can't handle the staring. I shift my vision to another part of the room . . .

There is only one man in the room other than the large-large man staring at me. He's a man without a face sitting on a chair in the corner behind a bushy plant. When I say he doesn't have a face I mean he hasn't any facial features at all, a blank man, hairless, poreless, no eyes or holes whatsoever, just a smooth man-shaped blob of meat.

"Don't be afraid," says the large-large man, eating a sandwich. "I won't hurt you."

I don't believe him. The man is house-sized, his face exploding out of his head, lion claws for cheek bones, razor-sharp whiskers.

"I like sandwiches," I tell him, the words falling from one of the sloppy sections of my brain.

"Would you like some?" he asks.

"Yes," approaching him, flinching, trying not to look at the featureless man in the corner who is speechless but pulsates in elbow ways.

"How much?" the man says as he pushes a button on his hand to create a quiet hum, and he pulls a new sandwich out of his sandwich, handing it to me fresh and dripping.

"Just a little," I say, but a whole monster-meat sandwich is already in my lap.

"Are you Cocoan? Whyrie's young husband?"

"Yes, I don't like my name," I tell him.

"She loves the younger men! How old are you again?"

"Twenty-five," I tell him.

"Now that's something, I'll drink to that," the man says, his beard larger than my arm when he swigs a bag of wine.

"Is she your friend?"

"I'm sorry," he says. "I never introduced myself, my name is Jesus Christ Mulligan."

My eyes cringe at him, and he continues:

"Yep, Jesus Christ, named after the almighty son of God, my parents were Christians but they were a little sick in the head if you know what I mean, you have to embrace a name like Jesus Christ though, otherwise you'll grow up pretty unhappy, so that's probably why I'm the religious studies professor down there at the university under the ocean, the one they're always remodeling, you know what I'm talking about?"

I shrug my shoulders into my neck. "Is she your friend?"

"I knew her since the beginning," breaking to drink more wine, "but I'm sure you know from Whyrie we're not allowed to talk about the project, everyone always has to keep things on the hush-hush-hush, and oh my God are you lucky to be married to that woman!"

TEN

I'm inside of my head again.

My mind is trying to escape the overwhelming company of Mr. Jesus Christ Mulligan, who doesn't seem to notice when I crawl away from our conversation to the comfy couch in my brain.

I just hate being around social people like Jesus, the ones who can't stop talking can't handle being alive without a conversation in the works. I wish I could just kill him, but I guess that's not possible anymore . . .

Death by murder isn't actually fatal these days. Just death by old age works. The scientists, years before Whyrie's time, discovered a cure for death. It works on all flesh that is not withered beyond repair. All diseases are curable as well.

People die all the time now that there is a cure for death, they just aren't as careful with themselves as they used to be not too scared of dying. Even I have died once a few years ago. I was electrocuted in a lightning storm, our whole block was fried when an arrow of lightning struck the water, blowing houses right off of their floatation devices, sinking to the bottom of the ocean. Many died that night, some even died permanently, lost under the waves, carried off by sharks. But most people were saved, revived, I guess I was one of them. Whyrie and I were not married at the time but were engaged, living in separate homes. She found my corpse floating down the road limp like a blanket my water legs keeping me from sinking.

I don't remember anything but that's how the story goes. I was just standing on my porch painting fish scales on my naked skin and the storm wasn't even that bad waves weren't even crashing in and then out of nowhere I was dead.

I sometimes remember the pain of dying . . . Not the pain of being killed by lightning but the pain of having my soul ripped out of my body, every fabric of lifeforce severing away from the flesh. It is something awfully upsetting, feels like a blackened banana filled with ants and a finger . . .

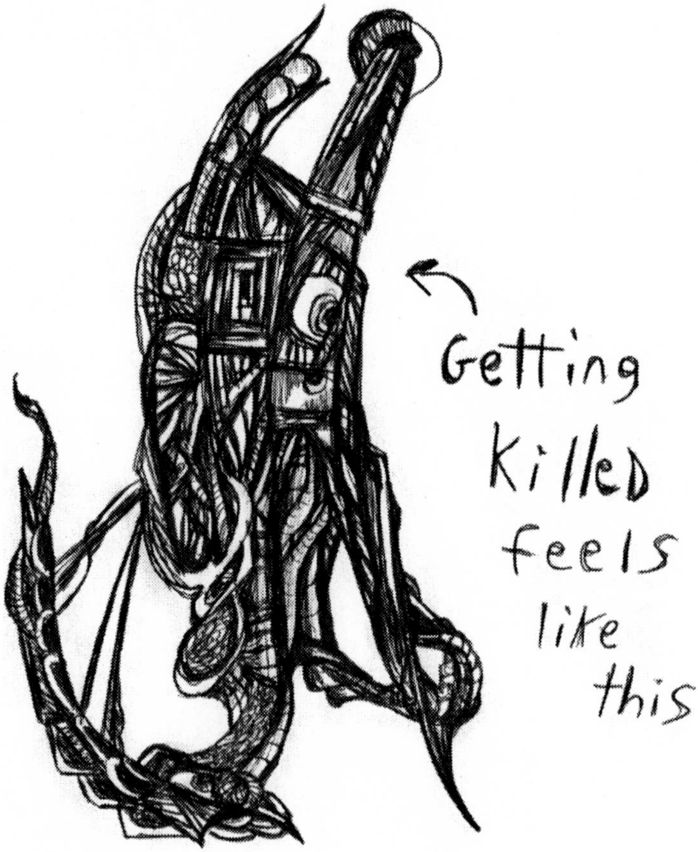
Getting killed feels like this

ELEVEN

Dinnertime —>

We're at the expensive place with the glass floor where you can see all the sharks goggle-swimming, chasing after fish and menstrual blood. And our table is in a private section because Whyrie wanted it that way. This would have been fine by me, I love privacy, but she has brought company along with her.

It was supposed to be my treat after sitting around waiting for her all day and what does she do? Invite all her co-workers. She knows how I dislike co-workers.

Here are their names:

Ni Gonzo
Sherry Vanne
Snow Fockly
Mark Looselef
Rufus Sumpticoff
and Mr. Jesus Christ Mulligan

Sherry is a woman I have already known for years, a woman much older than Whyrie but much younger in appearance and attitude, who was once my psychologist before I married Whyrie. A scared woman with spiderweb breasts and melty plastic clothes, cold-blooded, selfish, very nice to me though, and she walks her large pet goldfish like a dog down the street by her apartment.

They are all speaking chaotically, excitedly around the table passing large plates of black spiky food to one another and I'm curling down in my seat.

Ni Gonzo is the big leader of conversation, a real scary-looking man who opens his mouth into a wide circle to take bites of food. He doesn't have many friends but is sure popular at this table. I've never met him before this but Whyrie always tells me what an asshole he is, a real butt-plug.

I draw a tiny picture of Ni Gonzo, the picture my brain translates him to look, on my napkin with some fishy black goo from my dinner plate. Whyrie is sitting next to me, holding my leg, pretending the rest of me is not here, and Jesus Christ Mulligan is like an outsider too, but his presence is not entirely ignored.

Ni Gonzo soon sees my eyes looking to him, from him, to him, from him, and catches me in the act, though he pays no interest in my squidy drawing of him. He seems more interested in my presence, as if he has just noticed me for the first time this evening.

"Well," he says in a constructive tone, "what do you think, young man?" and Whyrie squeezes a fist on my leg.

"What do I think about what?" I ask him.

"Coming with us," he tells me, everyone with faces on me and my neck sweating hands brushing hair out of my eyes holding in my stomach.

"Coming with you?"

"He doesn't know anything about it," Whyrie tells him.

An evil grin at my wife, "You're taking him with us and you haven't told him what we're doing?"

"He doesn't need to know," she says.

"Know what?" I ask.

"He sure seems curious to me," he tells Whyrie. To me: "Do you know about what your wife does, son?" like I am a little boy.

I look down at my hands.

"Do you know why we are celebrating here tonight?" Ni Gonzo smiles with perfect teeth.

I shake my eyes back to him, "You're . . . going to spin a penny on the table top."

They pause, thoughts wandering, looking at me . . . and then the table opens into roars of laughter, fists banging on the table, especially Ni Gonzo and his stooges, Mark and Rufus.

"Yes," says Ni Gonzo, holding back his giggles. "Yes, something like that . . ."

"He's a barbarian," Jesus whispers to me, eating a claw-arm larger than my wife.

Whyrie looks at me with tears in her eyes and I have no idea why. Her face is sagging and red, looking at me as if I've just died, she probably looked at me that way when she found me dead in the water-street after I was struck by lightning.

I kiss her on the cheek and smile, wishing her sad face would go away.

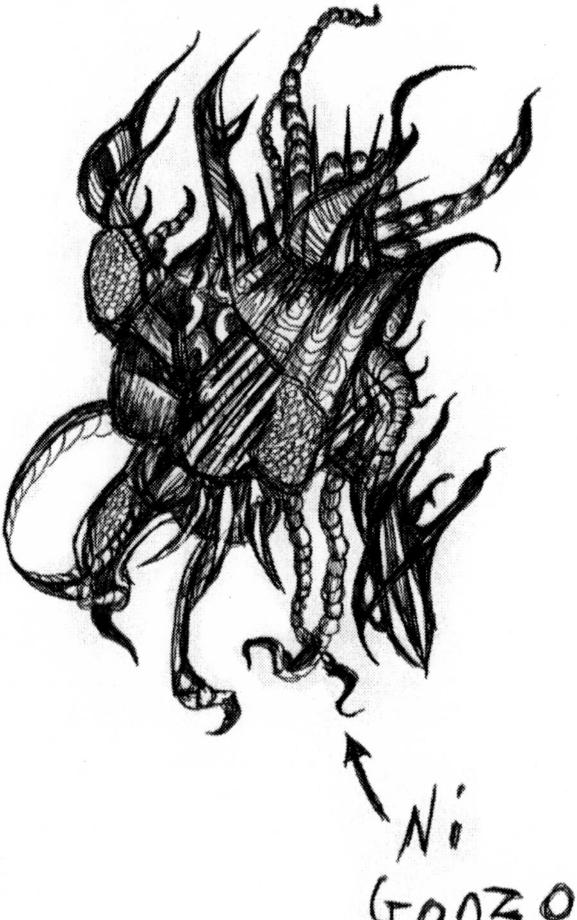

TWELVE

"Do you believe Jesus Christ was the messiah, Cocoan?" Ni Gonzo asks me, a hypnotic tone this time without a bit of giggling.

"Yes," I say, quietly like this is only between the two of us. "Do you?"

"I'm a scientist," he says. "I believe in facts, not magic, not God."

"Just because you don't understand God," says Jesus Christ Mulligan, "It doesn't mean He is not a fact."

I open my mouth and pause until Ni Gonzo

looks at me again.

"I don't think it matters whether or not there is a God," I tell him, "I believe in him because it is fun. I'd rather there be a God in the sky than just emptiness."

"But what if we could travel through time — spin a coin on a table — and prove whether or not Jesus Christ was the messiah. What would you say about that?"

"I'd say it sounds boring," I tell him.

And Whyrie digging into my thigh. "It sounds *amazing*," she tells me, correcting me.

"Why does it matter?" I ask them, wine must be kicking in.

"Because," Ni Gonzo says. "I feel we've been lied to. We need to find out for sure whether or not Jesus exists."

"Think about it, Cocoan," Sherry says in her soft voice. "Look all around you. What do you see? We are all messiahs." Sherry takes a sip of harsh steamy drink, and points to Mr. Mulligan. "Look at our Jesus, sitting next to you. He is no different than the Christ he was named after. He can walk on water. He can cure the sick. He can raise the dead. He can feed the masses."

"You see, Cocoan," Ni Gonzo says, "We don't just want to travel back in time to see if Jesus Christ was really the son of God or not. We are more interested in proving the theory that Jesus Christ was a time traveler from our age, who used our technology to trick the primitive people into believing he was the son of God."

"But why would anyone do that?" I ask Ni Gonzo. "Why would anyone from our world feel the need to parade around as the messiah?"

"That is a question you'll have to ask him yourself," says Ni Gonzo, re-filling a glass of wine by pushing a button on his finger.

PART TWO

Time Smell

ONE

I don't like it when Whyrie hides from me, always up in her study drinking by herself and working on something that requires my absence. We are scheduled to go into the past in a week. We are going to spin a coin on a table and then disappear into history, into the bible.

Maybe on our return, we will discover ourselves written in history books or maybe even the new testament or perhaps Ni Gonzo is right . . . Perhaps someone from our world was Jesus Christ, perhaps one of us travelers will become the Jesus Christ, such as Jesus Christ Mulligan. Maybe he was (will be) the messiah and nobody knows it, not even him. Perhaps he knows enough about the messiah to do everything correctly. Perhaps he will be killed on the cross, resurrected by one of the doctors and then brought back to our world, just after he says goodbye to his apostle-friends who plan on writing a book about him and changing the world for everyone.

Whyrie won't come downstairs to fuck me, even though I am down here waiting for her. Sometimes I'll wait hours and hours and she will not come down. Other times she just loses interest and goes to sleep without fucking me even though she promises she will, she pets my head and says she will screw me if I keep real quiet and wait downstairs for her but she is up there working all the time. I bet she is masturbating, thinking about somebody else up there, somebody younger than me . . . She doesn't like to talk about us.

She likes to do her work alone in her room and she doesn't like to come downstairs for anything. But she likes sex with me much better than she likes talking to me, and she likes dominating/controlling me even better than she likes sex with me.

I spoke to Jesus Christ Mulligan on the phone the other day Whyrie told me to tell him she was busy and couldn't come to the phone as she rubbed lotion on her legs so he spoke to me instead with a nordic voice. He said he can't wait to go to the past. He is so excited to actually get to meet the real Jesus Christ, someone who seems like an ancestor to him. Perhaps Jesus really is a blood relative to Jesus Christ Mulligan, perhaps everyone is.

I sit in the corner of the living room, naked in the dark, wondering how horrible life will be if Jesus

Christ is really a fake, and there is no God, and what if all the magic in the world is just technology? Like showing fire to a caveman for the first time, like showing a gun to a child. That is a very dull thought. And kind of sad. I don't want to go but Whyrie won't let me stay won't let me swim in the ocean.

Jesus Christ Mulligan says I will be famous if I go back in time and talk to Jesus. He tells me that even though time travel is now possible only a select few will ever be able to experience it. Only scientists. Sight-seers and history-changers will not be permitted. I will probably be the only non-scientist to ever go back there and I know I'm going to hate it.

Tomorrow I think I'll tell them I refuse to go, maybe I'll threaten to tell everyone in the city about their project if they try to force me to go. Or maybe I won't bother to argue. Maybe Whyrie is fed up with me and wants to ditch me in the past. That's fine. I'll go swimming until I drown or let them crucify me for having buttons in my skin.

At least I don't have to go to work anymore, not since I married Whyrie. I'm becoming much more scared of the world, much more trapped in my skull-dreams, but at least I don't have to work, and I think Whyrie prefers me this way.

This is
How
Whyrie's
Vagina →
tastes

TWO

Some teenagers are throwing a party out in the waves. They have a floating fire out there and are drinking whiskey, the gross pink kind that doesn't give you a hangover but is hard to take down and they are really punk-loud nearby our house at the shore.

On the balcony.

I see a couple embracing, a guy and a girl, or maybe two girls, or maybe two guys with long hair, sucking each other's chests and shoulders as I used to do just a few of years ago when I was still considered a young one. No, never mind, they are a girl and a guy, not two guys, not two girls, the girl wrapped around him so nicely that his gender is mistaken for hers at times and they are rolling around in the waves like a giant bouncy water bed.

The other teenagers ignore them and drink and throw limbs in the air.

Pity they aren't both girls making love out in the waves. Girls are much more passionate when they are in love together, and it lasts longer too I think. It seems like it would. Men and women just don't seem like they go together well. Like cats being with dogs. They are two different species trying to crossbreed.

Sometimes there are two women out in the waves, or two men. This is not unusual, or unnatural. We are taught not to think these things are unusual/unnatural. Gender, sexual preference, religious preference, race . . . there are no more prejudices anymore. (Well, except for maybe ugly people, poor people, dumb people, me . . .)

The most important prejudice to abolish was race, and many years ago they did it. It was done by a process called *Random Genes.*

You see, the problem that kept racism alive was that many people liked to group themselves socially, especially by race, because it was more comfortable, more familiar. People interacted within their race and that was that. So the government enforced Random Genes, a micro-program inserted into male testicles to alter their sperm so that every single one was different, by hair color, skin color, body type, sexual orientation, you name it. And eventually every family across the planet became multi-colored, and people grew to live with all races, within their own home, and races stopped separating themselves from other races, because they were comfortable/

familiar with being around one another.

It didn't happen overnight and child abuse was a real issue in some parts of the world for a while, but in the long run we were cured of racial prejudice for good.

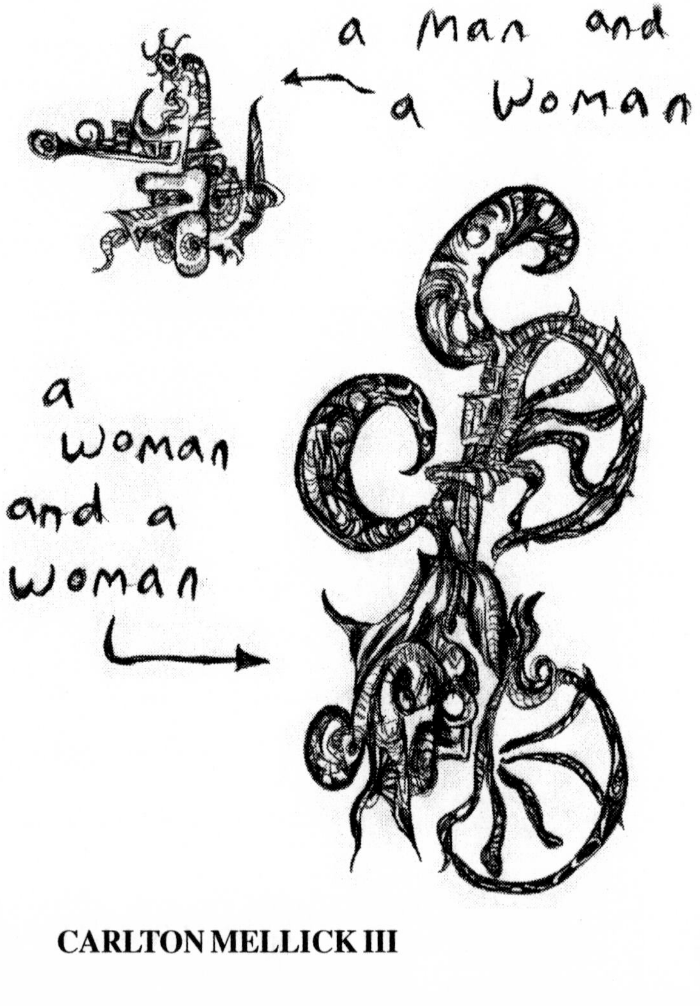
a man and a woman
a woman and a woman

THREE

The lobster kings are out in the streets again, crawling out of the ocean onto our sidewalks like rats in the city pinching at people's legs as they walk to the store.

Whyrie doesn't like to go outside while the lobsters are out so she works in her study instead of going to the lab and makes me go out to buy things for her.

The sun is smearing across the landscape, melting egg yolk, and it seems quite unfriendly to look at right now, my eyes concentrating on lobster-dodging. Then I hear screams and clutter-voices echoing down by the shops.

People are rioting, picketing signs outside of the city hall, bobbing up and down on the water street. Ni Gonzo is there, on a stage, waving fists at everyone. And he seems almost like a mad preacher up there, telling them about Christ and how he was a fraud and how he is going to prove it.

The people are holding up signs at him, telling him he will go to hell, thinking he will do something bad to Jesus when they meet in history, like kill him or make him sick, and then Jesus will never exist. His notions that Jesus Christ is someone from our time upsets them, makes them want to throw rocks at him, crucify him.

I wave to him from behind the crowd because it seems like something friendly to do, but everyone gives me evil looks and I begin to feel it would have been best to ignore Ni Gonzo and keep walking. The crowd waves their picket-signs at me too, now.

"There is another one of my travelers, over there," Ni Gonzo says in a mighty voice, pointing to me. "Bring him over here and he will help explain."

And the crowd embraces me with kicks and punches the security pulling me away from them dragging me onto the platform and the people are red-screaming enraged. As if I'm responsible for the death of their children.

"You might as well be responsible for the death of our children!" one particular healthy woman says to me. "Interfering with Jesus' life will be the end of us, as well as the end of our immortal souls!"

"I don't know," I tell them, awkwardly on stage.

And Ni Gonzo has disappeared all of a sudden, the security gone as well, leaving me alone to calm the angry mob.

"It's all stupid," I tell them. "They're never going to find Jesus anyway . . ."

But the crowd is in such a frenzy they don't have time to listen to me.

"It's just waste of time," I mutter.

They are concentrating hard on marching in perfect circles and chanting catchy and creative things and waving protest signs that say "The truth of Jesus Christ is not a science experiment" and "The proof is in our hearts" and "Time travel = Satan" and stuff like that.

FOUR

Ni Gonzo runs into me at a bar late at night, and he sits down next to me as if we were supposed to meet there, as if to say sorry I'm late I got caught up with something really important that you wouldn't understand. And he pats me on the shoulder and orders a drink that forces me inferior to him, something strong enough to make me go dizzy at the thought of taking it down, and this man can just pound the stuff, this man who does not seem to have a flaw, the best at everything, the strongest, almost engineered instead of born.

"Are you ready for the expedition?" asks the man, his mustache looking at me funny.

"I don't know," I tell him.

"We are on the verge of becoming immortal, you and I."

"I'd rather not be."

"You're very depressing."

"I'm going to sit here and drink and try not to be depressing. I'm also drinking so that I can forget that I have to travel back in time in a few days."

"Listen to your words," he tells me. "You sound like a machine. Say something exhilarating!"

"I'm not comfortable with exhilarating."

FIVE

There were zombie sharks flying through the air yesterday while my telepaceiver was turned off. They flew through town, eating flying fish, and I looked down at my hands and back at the flying sharks tearing away at their captured meals. And then I saw Ni Gonzo's assistants, Mark and Rufus, across the street. They were standing underneath the flying zombie sharks, standing in their shadows, but the two were off in their own worlds and did not acknowledge anything around them, not me, not the sharks. They just stood there calmly, eating sea-salads, facing each other, ripping into crunchy vegetables and dripping milky goo onto the sidewalk.

Streams of blood fell out of the sky and spotted Mark's white lab coat with sticky red circles. He continued eating, covered in blood and it made me wonder what the Virgin Mary was thinking all those years ago when God entered her to put His son into her, splitting her open without any blood . . .

SIX

I decide to take a boat out into the ocean, a sailboat that is fast and fun and Whyrie is too busy to notice me taking it out, can't stop me so I get away. I go to an island I know of that is a half hour from home. It is forbidden to go there, because it is a natural preserve I think, but nobody comes by this place, everyone forgets that islands exist now that we can live on water, making artificial islands.

I walk barefoot and the sand is spicy. It feels like gravity is much stronger here, making me want to lie down and let the blood trickle into my back.

The island is almost bare, you can see all the way across, it's only a square mile, and has only a little bit of grass and bushes to clothe it.

The sand is nice and I smile a lot.

Sometimes I come here and make a woman out of sand. I'll bring a wig, or a collection of Whyrie's hair found lying in corners, and make the sand woman look more human, bring some clothes for her, use little rocks for her nipples, and sometimes I make love to her so passionately that she falls apart, back into the beach.

Whyrie doesn't know about my affairs with the sand women, can't smell perfume on me or anything but seaweed and dirt, but she is still mad at me for sneaking away like that, cold at the thought of me running off in the ocean without her nearby, just in case I die again or am having fun. Sometimes she kisses me on my return, worried and glad I'm home, sometimes she hits me and locks me out of our bedroom.

The sand begins crawling into my pants packing itself up around the inside of my thighs tickling and saying hi to my crotch. I roll over and give it a kiss and let the ocean waves purr me into rest, into solemn dreamworlds of goodness.

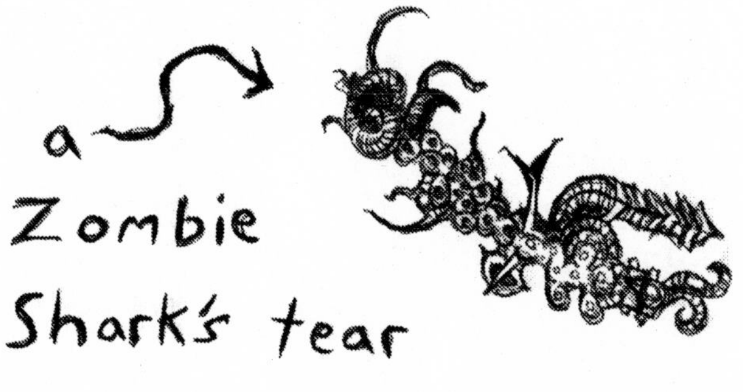
a
Zombie
Shark's tear

Ugliness World

SEVEN

"I refuse to go," I tell Whyrie. "The past is a cold, hard place."

"You don't have a choice," she says, brushing her mean hair, dark like burnt wood.

"You don't need me there, I'm not a scientist genius."

"Look," Whyrie stares at me through the mirror reflection, "we've already decided that you will go. I took Snow off the project so there would be an opening for you. She's in Pacifica taking pictures of mutant seals just for you."

“Then call her back here,” stomping my feet so that the house wobbles, “I’m not going anywhere.”

And I get out of the room before she has a chance to hit me.

I feel like
this when sailing

EIGHT

I'm at the local pub again, the one that floats in the air and circles and circles over this section of Ocean City, drinking and wondering when Whyrie will find me.

The place is pretty empty, which is quite uncommon for a floating bar. Sky bars travel from rooftop to rooftop so you don't ever need to walk to or from the place, it picks you up and takes you with it and you can drink and sing all across the sky.

I am trying to translate something from my

brain to a drawing on napkins, but the words are very difficult, can't really find English meanings to attach to them.

The snoring ones in the kitchen are not much help to me, they are lying on the counter and the floor, in the broom closet, and they are just out cold drunk waiting to be dropped off at home, and the bartender has bottles stacked on top of them, mummifying them in whisky bottles, and there is a man from Ireland at the bar puking on his dad, not really noticing me or anyone else, and his dad is also Irish and asleep, rust-snoring, arm dangling into broken glass. The bar shifting side to side makes the Irish man puke some more onto the floor or onto his dad or into a collection of jars.

"How is Ireland?" someone asks the Irish man, but the Ireland native spits tobacco at him, the illegal kind, and grunts at everyone in the room one at a time.

Ireland burned to the ground a while back. Nobody knew it at the time, but the whole country was flammable. It was made out of gasoline and lighter fluid I think. Many-many-many people burned to ashes. It was a very sad time to be alive.

All the survivors moved away from Ireland because they couldn't handle the idea of rebuilding on its charred corpse, couldn't look at it without crying. So they spread themselves all over the globe, to cities in Atlantica, Pacifica, Europe, America, Asia, Africa, Antarctica, Australia.

Sometimes a group of survivors will get together once a year to cry and sing sad songs about Ireland. And I wish I could do something to help but I can't because they don't want anything from me. I know they don't, I sometimes ask them —> "Hey, if you're going to build Ireland back up, I'll help out. Just give the word, and I'll help out." But they just grunt at me and spit goo-tobacco all over

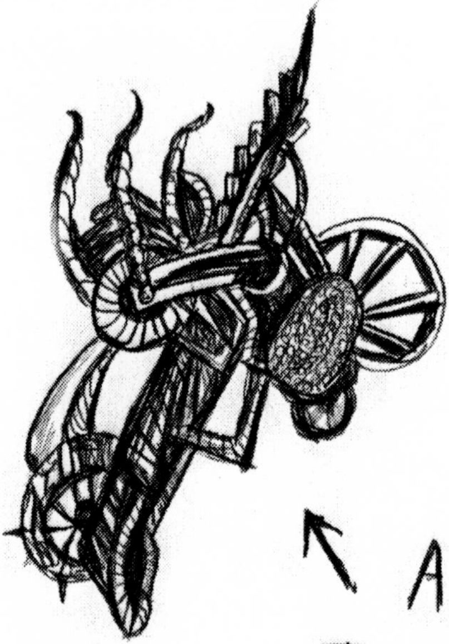

An
Irish
Drinking
Song

the place. Sometimes they like to punch things.

But a lot of people are less compassionate than me and say rude things like, "Hey, how's Ireland?" because they know how painful it is for them to think about their burned-away home.

Jesus Christ Mulligan (who is not Irish) boards the floating bar/ship while I am concentrating on my napkin. He is too large to get through the aisle and has to step over chairs and snoring ones to get across the bar to the dark corner where he sees me drinking.

I know he is there, but I continue to ignore him, my eyes glancing from peripheral point of view, his loud steps to me, and it seems he is making the ship rock from side to side, making the Irishman puke on his dad even more.

"This is totally absurd!" Mr. Jesus Christ Mulligan screams at the bar-attenders, shaking his belly at everyone as he laughs drunkenly though he is sober.

He squeezes himself into the booth with me, his arms fold and take up the whole table, brushes my napkin illustration right to the floor to a place I can't reach and he speaks: "Cocoan, you're here, we've been looking for you all over town, Ni Gonzo and I, we understand you don't wish to go to the past with us, is this correct? you are the seventh passenger, there is room enough for seven, it would be a waste, and we are leaving first thing tomorrow!"

"I don't need to go."

"Oh, but you must! it will be such a wonderful journey, we will see the world before there were engines or guns or equality, we will see the world when it was tender and raw, violent and fresh."

"I'm not interested."

"We will be able to find out whether or not Jesus Christ was real or fake! and if he is real, which I know he will be, we will meet him face to face, *the*

Jesus Christ, the son of God, and get to speak to him, won't that be amazing? won't that make you feel special? do you know how many people would kill for the chance to meet the holy savior?"

"I don't think I could handle meeting him if he were real. I wouldn't know what to say."

"Even if you said nothing," screams Mr. Mulligan, "even if you see him from a distance, it's worth the journey."

"I'm staying, Mr. Mulligan," my face trying to be as strong as possible, "and no one is going to convince me otherwise."

Jesus shrugs, glances at his shoes. Sighs.

"Well, what can I say?" he tells me. "If you want to miss the chance of a lifetime, which you will be doing, that's your problem."

"I wouldn't have any problems at all," I say, "if everyone in the world would just leave me alone."

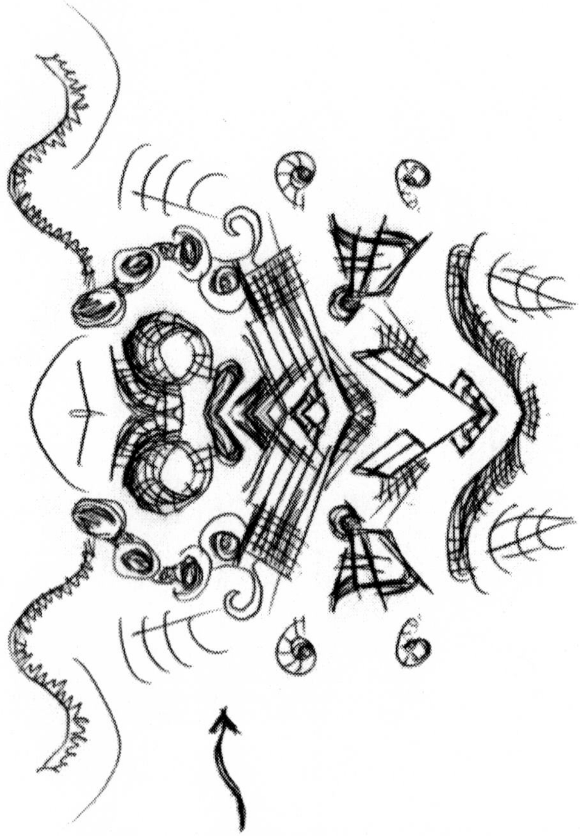

I have this
taste in my mouth

NINE

I'm hungover and naked, downstairs thinking about doing the exercises Whyrie always tells me to do, but I just fondle the plants down here instead.

There are worms swimming in the air near the plants, eating soil particles and swimming around my head, sometimes sticking to my skin to shrivel my nerves and make me jump.

Whyrie steps down the staircase with machine-precision, her clothes like someone from the time of Christ.

"Get dressed," she tells me, my butt facing her, red from sitting on splintery wood, patterned fabric.

"I am not going, I told you."

Whyrie tightens her lips, eyes closing to exhale.

"You can at least see me off," she tells me.

"I'm not going to fall for it," I tell her. "You're going to trick me. You're going to probably drug me. I'll fall asleep and wake up inside of the bible."

"You're such a shit," she tells me, stepping into the kitchen.

My skin crawls, and another worm flies near my nose, I watch my stomach breathe. I begin to feel alone.

"Fine," I tell her. "I'll see you off, but I'm still not going into the past with you."

There are clicking footsteps in the kitchen, but she doesn't respond.

I rub a worm out of my ear and place it into a potted plant, watching it dig deep underneath the surface, to mate with itself.

traveling

TEN

Under the water, traveling to the teleport station, bubble car going extra slow today, probably on purpose.

Whyrie's eyes are soft brown; they are always soft brown when she is sad. Normally they are a light color, like green and orange and gray, but they get really dark when she is sad.

"You really want me to go, don't you?" I ask her, my hands folded across my lap, keeping my distance from her.

"It doesn't matter."

"But you're really upset with me, aren't you?" I ask, pinching her nipple.

"You're better off staying here. It is dangerous where we're going. I don't want you hurt."

"That's my point exactly!" I tell her. "You want me to go so that I don't get into trouble here. You want me to go so that you can keep an eye on me. But it is much more dangerous in the past and I'm much more likely to get into trouble there."

"Just forget it," she tells me.

I smile, turn to the zombie sharks floating underwater, rotting, eating the flesh of the living fish.

"It's just . . ." Whyrie begins.

A doll's severed hand is floating in the water with the sharks.

"It's just what?" I ask, turning back to her sad eyes.

"Never mind."

"Just tell me. It drives me insane when you

do that."

"The reason I wanted you to go wasn't to make sure you stay out of trouble."

My eyebrows curl.

She stops the bubble car, allowing it to bob in its place, allowing the zombie sharks to circle us a few times. Then Whyrie faces me, her face loose and friendly.

"Cocoan," she says, "this is the first time anyone has ever traveled this far back into time before. We have done tests, going back a few minutes, an hour, but we've never gone thousands of years into history, not even a single year, not even a single day."

I sigh, give her my *you've told me this before* face.

"We don't know what exactly will happen," she says. "There's a chance we might not be coming back."

I break eye contact, go back to the sharks.

She continues, "If we were to get stuck there, I wanted you to be with me. We would be trapped in a primitive time, but we would still be together. And I think the only thing left to do would be to make love to you, raise a family, because that's all there is to do in that world."

There is a pause.

I look awkwardly to the sharks and to my fists and to the severed doll hand in the water.

"It's too late for me to go?" I ask.

"You're not prepared, and I don't have time to prepare you."

She pops the bubblecar into drive and continues toward the teleport station.

"I want to go with you," I tell her.

"I want you to go too," she tells me, concentrating on the water. "Especially since there is a good chance of death."

She looks at me and smiles breath-passionately, then back to the water to dodge a school of fish.

"I really want you there if that's the case," she tells me. "If I die, I want you to die with me. I can't handle the thought of you living on without me, by yourself, or with another woman. I couldn't handle that. You shouldn't be allowed to survive me at all. It makes me sick to think about it."

My hold cuddles her knee and my smile reflects into her, but the lips attached to Whyrie's face are closed tight again, her eyes no longer deep brown. Holding the wheel so firmly that her knuckles turn white.

God Whispering

ELEVEN

Teleport station:

I go with Whyrie through the teleport system to modern day Israel —> a cluttered little place with spade-roofs and hovering shopping malls in the clouds.

We are in the middle of a clearing, in Galilee, a landmark said to have been visited by Jesus Christ at some point during his travels. They have no idea if Jesus Christ will be in Galilee or not, but it seems like an intelligent place to start. Jesus Christ Mulligan said it would be best to start in Jordan, because that is where he will most likely be during the time of our arrival, but Ni Gonzo doesn't listen to Jesus Christ Mulligan. I think he is prejudiced against fat people. If Whyrie hadn't insisted, Mulligan would never have been a part of the project at all.

"I want to go," I tell Whyrie. "What if you never come back?"

"It's too late now. We don't have supplies or clothes for you to come. It's your fault for refusing."

"Why didn't you tell me you might not be coming back?"

Whyrie goes into her pack to fidget with things.

"He can still come if he wants to," Ni Gonzo says, in the background setting up a splintery old table.

"Do we have enough rations for him?" she asks.

He nods, turns to one of his assistants. “Mark, multiply the rations before you seal up your control panel.” Then Ni Gonzo says to Whyrie, “His modern clothing style is going to be a problem, though.”

“Yeah,” an assistant, Rufus, says to me, “if you want to go, you’re going to have to travel naked.”

“I can’t go naked!” I say to them.

“We didn’t have time to get extra clothes made,” says Ni Gonzo. “They had to be stitched by hand to look authentic, which took several months. There are no extras.”

“Once we get there,” Rufus says, “we will get you some clothes from the closest native. You’ll only be nude for a few hours at most.”

“I can’t go naked, give me something, anything.”

“He’s shy,” Whyrie tells them. “Before I met him, he wouldn’t even shower in the nude.”

A snicker from one of the assistants.

"Sorry," Ni Gonzo says. And then he yells to Sherry in the background, "Five minutes."

Whyrie strips me of my clothes and I just stand here inching my feet back and forth. She covers up the buttons in my flesh with skin-colored putty, so now I can't walk on water anymore. She kisses my neck, but doesn't smile and pretends to ignore my nakedness.

TWELVE

We gather around a table in the middle of the clearing, my naked skin shivering in the breeze ticklebumps creeping I'm covering my private parts as best as I can with two hands. Whyrie holds my shoulder firmly, loving me, just in case we don't survive the trip backwards.

I realize the faceless man is with us. The blank blob of meat that was in the waiting room when I met Jesus Christ Mulligan, the scary mound of flesh person. It is just standing there with us, wrapped in a large robe as a disguise, its egg-smooth face shining through the robe-opening at me.

"Ready everyone?" Ni Gonzo asks.

Everyone is silent.

I try to ignore the faceless man.

Ni Gonzo reveals a small round device, the size and color of a penny but much more shiny, textures like the inside of a computer, and it makes a clicking noise as it touches the table top.

The coin-like contraption begins to move, spin, circles, all by itself. Ni Gonzo's eyes light while Whyrie's eyes close shut, snowy eyelids flickering.

And then some colors spray all over us, some liquid-like gas-goo splashes onto our faces, arms, some on Whyrie's breasts, my naked chest. Everything around us seems to disappear for a while we seem to get sucked inside of the coin's spinning motion become a part of the concept of time and lose all our flesh.

Inside of time there is this horrible smell. It is like smashed earwigs and burned rubber and black licorice. I want to plug my nose but my hands are scared to leave my private things . . .

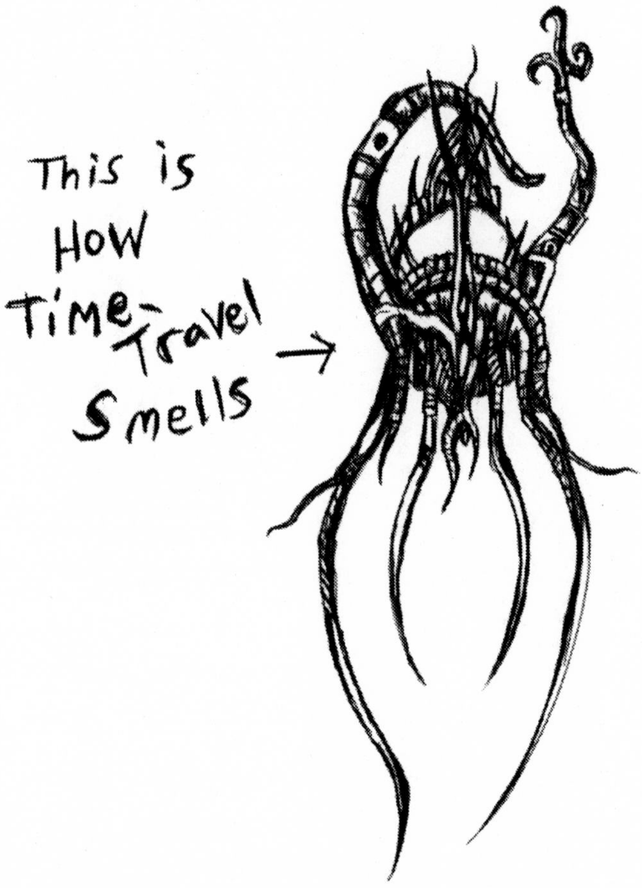
This is
How
Time-Travel
Smells

PART THREE

The Dirty Ones

ONE

I find out that my real name is Mr. Daniel Shoes.

My name isn't really Cocoan at all. Go figure. Cocoan is just a nickname that held on tight for a long time so long I forgot my original name. I guess it's not all that important to be called Cocoan —> which is a very unpopular name that means *Somebody who Kills the Snails* —> but I am disappointed that I have been mistaken about my identity most of my life.

Time travel somehow cleared up some fuzzy memories. I now know things about me that had been completely buried over the years, hidden in greasy folds of brain meat. Like the time a black poodle walked on the sidewalk while I was playing hopscotch with a girl I liked, or the time I had beans and mustard for lunch and pretended it was cucumber pizza, or the time I read a book on lesbian pirates, or the time I was in bed and thinking about a vampire . . .

It's nice to remember these long forgotten experiences but they are quickly becoming a clutter to my brain storage, things not all that important that I threw away are now at the front of my mind again. All the waste in my memory's trashcan have been emptied out all over my head during the trip, messing up the place.

My thoughts feel soggy. Perhaps it's not good to remember so much . . .

TWO

It is much hotter in the bible for some reason. We are in the exact same place we were in the future but now everything is primitive and hot and bland. My head is foggy. There are people all around me looking at me screw-funny eyes all over me. My hands are my only clothing but the natives don't seem to be too clothed themselves.

And they scare me.

Nobody else from the future is here. Just me with porcupine-eyed people at me. I don't know why I'm alone. I'm a little disoriented I guess. My hands feel like they each have one finger too many.

And it feels like God is whispering into my left ear . . .

Whyrie is off in the wilderness, I think. I heard her say something to me, but I'm not sure. I wasn't very conscious at first. She possibly ended up in a different time but I don't know how time travel works. I shouldn't think about that, it is far too depressing, and all these people keep looking at me! I can't handle it I wish everyone would just leave me alone or at least give me something to wear. Should I ask? No, I don't want to ask anyone anything, not these people. I don't want any clothes anyway, I should make my own clothes . . .

I hear a cry out in the distance, a Whyrie-like cry, well a woman's voice but I've never really heard Whyrie cry out so it must be her. I charge to her and make sure nobody looks at my backside as I run, my flesh is all jiggly and people are going to laugh, watching for thorns on the ground. My feet are so soft and fragile . . .

In the past
everything smells
like this

THREE

I see Sherry and Ni Gonzo's assistants, Rufus and Mark, behind some rocks, and they are all huddled together.

"What's wrong?" I ask, too quiet for anyone to hear.

Then I notice —> Sherry glass-crying, biting a branch. Her leg is encased inside of rock, a collection of pudgy boulders, up to her knee. The assistants try to free her, pulling her body, and they have no attention for Sherry's screams.

Eyes rolling into the back of her head . . .

"So how was that jumper?" asks one assistant.

"Nice, nice," replies another assistant. "I really enjoy thinking about removing my arms and legs, and drinking coffee from a sponge."

They treat the woman screaming in their arms as if she's a job they have to do and they'd rather not be doing it.

Sherry's leg goes deeper into the rock. Now it is up to her thigh, sucking her up inside of it. Pin-screaming, her eyes closed and she doesn't say a word, ignoring the assistants as much as they ignore her.

"What is wrong?" I ask.

"The mountain was made in Denver, but it was transported to Oceanview," an assistant says.

"No," replies the other, "I'm not much of an egg person, I like cheese bagels for breakfast with peach-cinnamon jelly."

Sherry sinks deeper, getting eaten away by the rock, or is something else eating her? Time itself might even be responsible.

When she teleported through time, she must have appeared in this era with her leg inside of stone. Sherry and the rock must be at war with each other battling over which is in its rightful location and a rock, in being a rock, is winning outright without much of a struggle.

"I wonder if butter has been invented yet," says an assistant.

They are now totally ignoring the crying woman, letting go of her arms as her other leg slurps into the smooth boulder surface, drinking up her lower torso.

Red/yellow screams pierce the landscape . . .

"I hope the food isn't too horrible here," says the other. "We're likely to get sick."

Sherry goes silent, her eyes close as if she

heads into comfortable sleep, her face sinking into stone until she's just a curling lock of hair in the breeze . . .

"Maybe we should start cooking something to eat now before it gets too late," says an assistant.

"Yes," says the other, "We seem to have lost many hours in travel. It should be dark soon."

And both of them walk away, wiping the stone fragments off of their palms and breathing in the fresh air.

Gazing the landscape —> all the primitives in the surroundings vibrate like computer-bugs.

FOUR

The people around here are cancer-disgusting, really sickly and filled with parasites and spiders and worms and they don't wipe themselves when they go to the bathroom, going to the bathroom wherever they want, inside their homes probably, their faces crooked and thin, most of them more bony than I've ever seen. Many cock-eyed. Deformed. Their flesh made out of squid-material. Looking at them, I don't see any life at all, no energy, no freewill. The living dead.

And they smell so horrible, like raw meat mixed

with Styrofoam.

Whyrie and Ni Gonzo have set up camp for the night, Jesus Christ Mulligan and the faceless man snapping fingers at each other in the shadows. And the assistants won't get out of my way so I can get to Whyrie, wobble-talking and moving too slowly, and some insecty person behind me is looking at me with knives for eyes, licking his eel-lips like I'm a woman or little boy perfect for raping.

"No clothes yet," Ni Gonzo tells me, attaching strips of meat to a stick. And Whyrie has not said a word to me yet sitting in white dirt and organizing a pattern in the rocks. Nobody has said a word about Sherry's whereabouts, wrapped up in their own concerns.

"This will be excellent!" says Jesus Christ Mulligan from shadows, clenched fists, and he waves me over.

I trudge around the campfire to the large-large man who sits next to the strange-strange man who has no face and Jesus is babbling **—>**"We must go to the lake and see if anyone knows where He is, maybe we will find the family of Peter and Andrew, or maybe John and James' family as well."

Freezing, the sun is going down and the temperature has gone from sweaty-hot to wind-chilling, standing there above Jesus Christ Mulligan and his buddy (the faceless man) who sits in a lifelike position though the creature seems far from alive **—>** more like a man-shaped glob of modeling clay.

"What is *he* doing here?" I ask Whyrie.

She is busy bobbing her head up and down.

"What do you mean by that?" Jesus Christ Mulligan tells me with an angry mouth. "You knew I was coming along . . ."

"No, no, no," I cry. "Not you."

"Sit down next to me," Mr. Mulligan says, brushing away dirt with his weathered hand to make a comfortable spot for my nude bottom, and I agree to sit next to him but I do not trust him with my nudity, nor anyone, especially the dirty ones over the hill who do not stop staring —> smiling crooked teeth like hyenas.

"I bet you're a little confused right now, aren't you?" he asks me. "Everything will be fine in the morning, but for now we are all a bit disoriented because our brains were shuffled up in transport."

"I thought it was just me," I tell him. "So Sherry wasn't really eaten by the rock?"

"Everything will be fine in the morning," his face smile-nodding, "but for now we are all a bit disoriented because our brains were shuffled up in transport."

And he continues to nod and smile at me . . .

FIVE

The sun is really bright in the morning, brighter than the sun over Ocean City. It feels like a blanket over me, closest thing I have for a blanket . . .

No one is here except for Whyrie —> coiled awkwardly around the campfire, crispy green bugs relaxing on her face.

Everyone else is gone. Not even the featureless clay man is here anymore.

I rise, hold my privates, staring off into the distance.

Figures stand on the neighboring hills, the shadowy dirty ones with squids for faces, just watching us, curious. All of them want to rape me, and there are more of them than before, just staring, curious, horny. Sometimes stretching their arms up to the sun in a snake-like dance.

"Wake up, Whyrie."

She is dead asleep, I hold her cold-bone shoulders, shake slightly. "Where is everyone?"

Whyrie groans, speaks muffled in the sand, spraying dirt across the weeds with her breath. "They went to go look for Jesus."

"Are we supposed to just wait for them?" I ask.

"No," her voice slowing. "We're supposed to go with them."

What?

"Wake up, Whyrie."

"Just go back to sleep," she tells me.

"But what about the others? Did they leave us?"

"It doesn't matter, just let me sleep some more. I'm trying to draw a picture . . ."

"Jesus Christ Mulligan said we were disoriented, they shouldn't have left us if we're disoriented."

"We're fine, we just need to sleep it off."

Pushing her again, "We need to find them, we can't get back without them. I don't want to walk around naked forever."

"Just go to sleep!" she wasp-whispers.

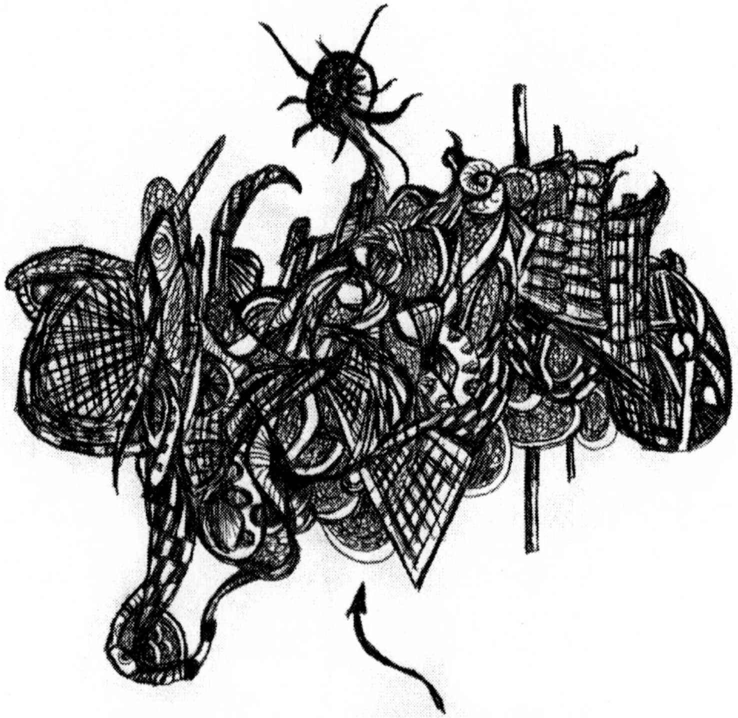

A Dirty
one

SIX

Whyrie wakes. As she rises, the people on the hills disband, walking away disappointed as if they were vultures wondering if my wife was departed flesh.

"Where did everybody go?" Whyrie asks.

"You said they went to look for Jesus," I tell her.

"Without us? What do they think they're doing?"

Whyrie gets her things together, packing up the camp with fast robot arms.

“Oh no,” she freezes, twitching eyeballs.

She gazes at me. “There’s a chance . . .”

“What?” I ask.

“No,” she says. “No . . .”

“What? What?”

“Their presence might not have held in this era. Time might have displaced them. Their atoms would be spread into millions of pieces. A tiny part of them in each and every second in history. And there’s a chance it could happen to us as well, at any time . . .”

“What are we going to do?”

“Hope they really did go to find the messiah,” she blows her seaweed hair from her face. “We might be stuck here forever.”

SEVEN

We search the land for a few days, no sign of the rest of our party, no clue to where we have been traveling.

For food, we have been eating snakes, stoning them to death from a distance and hanging them by sticks over a fire, or sometimes drying them in the sun for jerky to carry with us.

"Can you spare some clothes?" I ask a passing dirty man with many layers of clothing and red bulging eyes but he ignores, continues on his path.

"Only Jesus Christ Mulligan and Ni Gonzo can speak their language," Whyrie tells me.

There is a patch of shade ahead and we decide to rest, my skin agitated, uneasy with being unclothed. My feet are wrapped in plants and bark but that offers little protection, the skin ready to peel right off.

We sit away from each other, backs against separate rocks, watching the dirty ones pass us on the trails, all headed in odd directions. We have yet to find a town or village, but there are large crowds of deformed/smelly people all around us, just mindlessly wandering in the middle of the desert, zombiewalking in shredded clothing, not carrying any supplies at all, not even water. The roads have to lead to someplace, but we can't find civilization anywhere, and the people walking the roads just ignore us. We try to communicate but they just stare at my sandy naked skin.

Whyrie's hands are digging in the dirt, mechanical, nails clawing deep within.

"So do you want to have children with me?" I ask Whyrie.

She pauses, angry eyebrows. An exclamatory: "What?"

"You said you wanted to have children with me if we got trapped in this time. You said there would be nothing left to do but make love to me and make a family. That's why you wanted me to go, remember? Just in case . . ."

"Children? Here? *My* children?"

"But you said . . ."

"Never mention children with me," a handful of mud splattering onto my knee, "We're going to find the others and continue the study. We are NOT trapped here."

I wander my eyes away.

"Children . . ." Whyrie says, dirty-faced. "That's all we need . . ."

We sit in silence with each other, alone together.

For a minute, I hear Whyrie crying. Not from her eyes, though, but from deep inside of her. There is such a thing as bleeding internally. Well, Whyrie is *crying* internally, her tears dripping all over her lungs and liver and kidneys.

I begin to see her tears leak out of her arms, legs, neck, and back, through pores on her skin . . .

EIGHT

Walking again.

My feet are pretty bloody and numb, leaving a trail of skin like breadcrumbs. Whyrie isn't sure what to do about me, her wilderness survival skills all blank, her medical knowledge slightly disordered inside of her head.

"Only Ni Gonzo knows survival techniques," Whyrie says. "We must find him."

"But weren't you all instructed at the university last week?"

"Only Ni Gonzo will know how to fix your feet."

Swarms of dirty ones clog the landscape now, in all directions, all of them still staring at me, some of them stop in their tracks just to watch us.

"Is civilization close?" I ask her, and she slaps my words away like flies.

Many dirty ones are shambling at us, perhaps lepers who were shunned by their neighbors.

"It's a town," Whyrie says.

But I don't see anything, just dozens of diseased squid-people walking the road.

"Where?" I ask.

"In front of us."

—> Nothing.

Then her eyes go back to looking at the road, disinterested, our pace straggling and whitish/weak.

NINE

Through neighborhoods of shacks and horrible smells, wandering, eyes dried out of our heads and nobody to talk to.

A large-large dirty old man, larger than any of the other dirty ones, approaches us on the path, mumbling in some ancient language and making me sick with his scent.

"Go away," I tell him. "We don't understand you."

"Ah, you speak English," says the dirty old man. "I was just letting you know that if you need a free place to stay for the night there are many abandoned houses in this town here, many of us are leaving our wealth and our homes to travel north."

"How do you speak English?" I ask the large-large old man, large as a gorilla. "That's impossible."

"You might want to hurry up before the looters clean out every home," says the large old dirty man. His voice sounds very familiar. "Or maybe you are willing to go with us, to follow the messiah?"

"Nobody speaks English yet," I tell him, and Whyrie is staring at my feet, at all the rocks and bugs stuck inside of the wound.

"Good luck to you people then," he says. "I'll be on my way. I've been waiting twenty years for this day to come."

And the old large-large man begins to walk away.

"But where did you learn to speak English?" I

scream, the man waving a giant arm at me as he disappears into the crowd.

"He doesn't remember us," Whyrie says, shrugging her lips.

"Remember us?" I ask.

"Let's find a home," Whyrie says. "I'm tired of traveling."

PART FOUR

Messiah Mania

ONE

"It's been a year since the last time I turned on my telepaceiver," I say. "A year since we traveled into the past to become a part of history instead of the present, and Whyrie is seven months pregnant."

"Yes, I am," Whyrie says, smiling.

I guess I have been talking out loud instead of inside of my thoughts . . .

Anyway, we're living inside a beautiful abandoned house in a small fishing village on the coast of

Lake Galilee, and we make our living by selling items from our home era (that Whyrie still knows how to make) to the local primitives, and I go sailing and fishing for our food and Whyrie is really happy that the fish are so good, as if fish are better in this era than in Ocean City.

Our bodies are still capable of being messiah-like, walking on water and reproducing the food supply, but we promise not to use our special abilities unless absolutely necessary. We don't want to be burned as witches or messiahs, especially now that we have a child inside of Whyrie.

She smiles much more now that we are in messiah-world, maybe because she doesn't have as many responsibilities, less stress, and I am very happy as well. I was especially happy in the beginning when we would just lie around all day in an army of pillows and blankets, and Whyrie would climb on top of me whenever she got bored.

Now she is in love with her stomach and pets it all the time, smiling at me. She looks so cute with her bulging pot, and she laughs and puts her finger in her belly button, sometimes sleeping with it on top of me so that I can hear two heartbeats in my dreams.

"Aren't you eating?" she asks me, pointing at my fish.

"I'm sick of fish," I tell her.

And she crab-grabs it from my plate, still half a fishhead in her mouth.

"We're in Heaven," she says.

This is how I see my future

TWO

Outside on a hill —> basking in each other's odors amongst the dirty ones and Whyrie snuggles her head against her own stomach wraps my arm around her neck. She can't see because her eyes are closed but the horizon is lovely in a blood-red cockroach-clouds kind of way. There's no ocean underneath the sky which makes me think sad things but it is still really nice sitting here with the woman I love.

It is messiah mania. People are ranting about Jesus everywhere, whether they believe in him or not. I have not picked up the local language effectively, especially when speaking it, but I can tell when they are talking about Jesus because one person will have sparkles in the eyes and the other will be shaking the head *no no impossible how insulting*.

The civilization is very delicate, even breathing on it too roughly can do serious damage, and this rumor of the messiah is making everyone tense. Somebody yelled at me yesterday just for saying *Jesus!* when a giant spiky bug was crawling up my leg. I couldn't understand him, of course. But Whyrie knows the language now, mostly, and told me that the man said he would hit me if I spoke that name again. Even though Jesus isn't even pronounced the same way in their language.

"Should we go see him?" I ask Whyrie.

"No," she muffle-speaks to my lap, "Forget about him."

"Are you sure?" I ask.

"He's all trouble," Whyrie says.

THREE

The past seems flat to me, the people, the houses, the land, so bleak-empty and boring, like they are all just marionettes pretending to be real. The longer I stay here, the more unrealistic everything feels. Everything is made out of cardboard, two-dimensional.

I'm walking through town and wondering if Whyrie is really happy. I think she smiles because of happiness, but perhaps a smile means she is sad . . . She used to yell at me, hit me, in Ocean City, and though her eyebrows were curled and her mouth was frowned, it really made her happy to be so mean, and though she hurt me emotionally and physically I was still happy that she was happy. Now I begin to wonder —> What if she is really sad when she smiles? Maybe she is crying inside because she has no use in this world other than the raising of what is in her belly . . .

I sit into the dirt outside of a deserted pavilion which must have one time been filled with blacksmiths, rope makers, and other assorted craftsmen. Drawing a picture in the sand, trying to figure things out. There are people all around me talking about Jesus Christ and his miracles. I think they are raving about how he needs to be killed because he is an abomination and think crucifixion is necessary.

I agree with that idea.

Jesus, the messiah, is responsible for attracting us here. If it wasn't for him I would be back at home with the other water walkers and Whyrie wouldn't be smiling anymore, she would be happy instead of pregnant.

My face is smelly.

I can taste dirtiness in my nose, the skin covered with rotten odor from living in this barbaric community of dirty ones, red-sickening me, the sun melting the smell into my lips, stinging my eyes. I'm going blind with smell.

People standing all around me now, gathering, but I'm blind, can't see. They block out the sun by, leaning over to pick me up and take me away.

Her
warmth

FOUR

"There you are," someone says to me, "What happened to you? We've been looking for you for three days now."

I let my eyes focus out the sun and see Ni Gonzo, his two assistants, and the featureless man standing over me, fresh clothing on, clean-smelling. A little worn but still clean.

"Ni Gonzo?" I say.

"We've been looking everywhere," they say. "We got to get moving. I believe Jesus is at the end of his days. Are the others with you?"

"Only Whyrie," I tell them. "She's pregnant."

"Pregnant?"

"Pregnant, yes. It's been a year since we were separated . . ."

"A year?"

"I'll take you to Whyrie," I tell them.

FIVE

Whyrie isn't happy to see Ni Gonzo.

Her eyes shrink and her teeth bite her lips. "Where the hell were you?"

"We've just now found you," they say. "There's not much time . . ."

Whryie shakes her head at them.

"It's too late, Ni Gonzo," she says. "We're not going."

Ni Gonzo **—>** ?

"We've already built a life for ourselves here."

"The messiah is to be crucified soon," says

Ni Gonzo, "we don't have time for this. We need you. Especially now that you've been studying the culture for the past year."

"We've been trying to ignore the culture," I tell them.

"Either send us to Ocean City now or leave us alone," Whyrie cuddles her stomach. "We don't need you anymore."

And then she smiles at me.

She must be in such pain.

SIX

The newcomers, even more fresh than I remember them that day, decide to stay with us a single night, to see if a night of sleep will change Whyrie's mind.

Maybe it is a good thing we leave. Whyrie has been smiling too much in this era. She must hate herself. She must hate me.

There are flies inside of the house and on top of Ni Gonzo's head. The place is cage-cluttered with these people here. And the featureless blob of skin makes me tense as needles sitting at our table as if waiting for food and Whyrie gives him a fishhead but he doesn't eat anything, just sitting at a table like he's waiting for food . . .

Something of emotional significance catches my sight —> The world outside of our window is looking like volcanoes, fire and ash raining down, slow-silent and overlapping the country-scape, making my body convulse with its power, eyes stretching red-wide. Everyone looks out to see what I am seeing. They also become captivated by the fire storm outside of the window.

"Is it the messiah?" asks Rufus with a big nose.

"No, the messiah isn't like that," Ni Gonzo answers.

But it sure feels like a messiah. The radiance can be felt on my insides, and it is almost like Christmas with the ash raining down like snow. Perhaps it is Christmas everyday when Jesus is alive . . .

"How is the past?" an assistant asks Whyrie, I

think.

I think she responds, "It is like the present, but everything doesn't seem so flat and empty."

The volcanoes stare at me funny, just as paintings do when I look at them too long. The sun reflects off the moon. People are all over the ground with their stink . . .

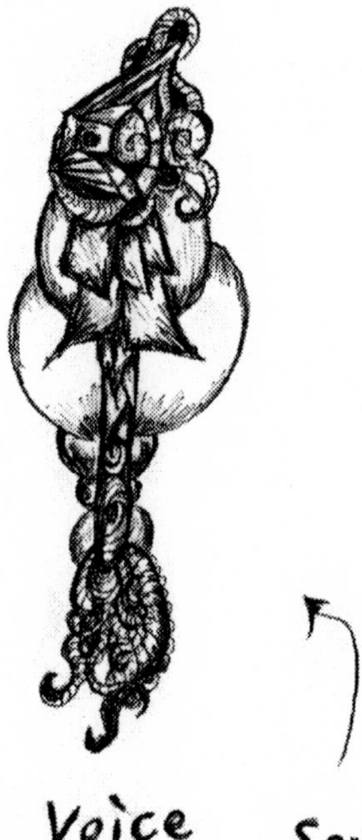

Ni Gonzo's Voice sounds like green-gray Mixed with this

SEVEN

"It would be best," Whyrie says, naked back to me, half-standing out of our glimey bundles of bed to Ni Gonzo, her breasts open to him as if it is nothing new. And I'm half-waking, against her cold butt. Dirt layers on the blankets between us.

Asleep.

Then awake again —> the assistants have left with Ni Gonzo, leaving their featureless blob-friend behind.

And Whyrie is against me in bed, no longer with smiles, her hands firm against my back but the rest of her skin still loose to me, conscious with eyes closed.

"We're going with them," she says.

My blanket rasping my forehead, warming up like a sickness.

"I thought we were going to stay?"

"I want to," she tells me. "But we don't belong here. I don't want our child to live in such a primitive world."

"But you love this world?"

"I love it because I am in control here," she tells me. "The people are fragile and like children. It feels good to be around them."

"So we are staying?" I ask. "I'll stay . . ."

"No, I said we're leaving."

"I'll leave," I tell her.

EIGHT

Following the trail of the messiah.

Whyrie and I have never traveled very far outside of the village before, staying indoors and keeping ourselves company, making a family, but now it is interesting to see the historical countryside. The people are hollow of knowledge, unaware their world is round, unaware of space, unaware they will someday be able to walk on water.

From city to city to city, dirty people give word the messiah had come and gone, they point in directions with crooked paper fingers. But Christ remains camouflaged, doesn't want us to find him.

Sometimes we even see a group of people inside of a town flocking together around someone, and they are all praising this someone, chanting the name "Christos," and telling us about what magical things he's just done over there, but by the time we get to the front of the crowd the messiah is gone, disappeared to another section of town, and everyone is charging to that part of town, and we go after him but he is gone when we get there also. He is at the edge of town, and we go there. But all of the people are settling down and going back to their homes and they tell us, "He has left," and they don't tell us where he has left to because we seem awfully suspicious and our featureless man looks like a demon from hell to them, or maybe a leper, or someone with a face-deteriorating disease, and so we don't get very far.

We go to another town, smelly and tired all day, camping outside in the trees and hoping to escape bandits and rapists and soldiers, the colors of this era are bland right now, the ground and people, nothing gets painted colorful it seems, and the artwork is supposed to be exquisite but it's all so boring and tired.

Another town proves the messiah has been there, and everyone is sad in this town, a town with green acorn-shaped rocks growing around a tree in the town center, but everyone is sad because a man named Lazarus, the man Jesus Christ raised from the dead, has been killed, dead for the second time.

Some of the townspeople, however, think it was awfully convenient for the undead man to become dead again . . . how many people actually saw this man undead? People are getting skeptical, wondering if Jesus is a liar. I guess some people are optimistic and others are pessimistic. Times are bad here. Everyone wants a savior everyone wants to be saved from something. But not everyone believes it is possible.

"We're *never* going to find him," I tell everyone.

. . . and they scratch at the grit in their pubic hairs . . .

NINE

Ni Gonzo is talking to a weird man up ahead —> a man or maybe he's an alien from the outer space with his metal eyes shiny silver eyes that reflect the sun at me and blind me his complexion pale and rubbery clean like no one else around him neatly pressed white clothes just standing there watching us arms crossed at us, and speaking about somethings to Ni Gonzo.

"He speaks English," Mark says to Rufus, awkward lips, avoiding contact with the man's silver eyeballs.

We can't understand what they are talking about but it is English and Ni Gonzo is smiling and almost hopping in small circles with every word that comes out of the strange man's mouth.

Ni Gonzo brings him to us, like an old friend he's known for several years.

"We've been tracking you for some time," the strange man says to the rest of us, a tangy robot accent. "You have to come with me."

"To where?" Whyrie asks, holding her belly.

"To Jesus Christ, of course," Ni Gonzo says, pink-giggled.

TEN

The man's wiry hairs twirl like electricity is flowing through them as he walks in front of me, his feet making perfect prints in the sand. I try to step in his perfect footprints, but my feet are too swollen and crusty to make a match, far too imperfect. He takes us deep into the vacant flatlands of this era, away from even the bandits and demons, to a hole in the ground.

We drop like a gaggle of Alices down the hole into an underworld of glass machinery, to an oval room that has its own sun hanging from the ceiling, a conference-type chamber, rusty-black and spiky.

About twenty other silver-eyed ones are gathered around a large melty table. The people here remind me of Whyrie, sitting very firm in their chairs, tight posture, shiny eyes stare-locked at us. Electrical people.

Our guide sits at the head of the table and introduces himself, "I am Philip Lottlin of the Atlantic Tribe."

"We are all of the Atlantic Tribe," says another man.

Ni Gonzo spiders his fingers, "Where is Jesus Christ?"

"There is no Jesus Christ," says Philip Lottlin. "There never was one."

"There has to be one," Rufus tells him.

"Actually, yes, there was a man named Jesus," says a higher voiced under-dweller. "Mary, the one known to you as the Virgin Mother, produced a son by the name of Jesus some time ago. But this boy died of drowning at the age of fifteen."

"He was not the messiah," says another.

I try not to let them see me yawn.

"Then who is the messiah?" Whyrie asks.

"There never was a messiah," says the underdwellers. "And there was never a God."

"You're the ones responsible for forging Jesus Christ?" says Ni Gonzo, smiling.

Philip Lottlin says, "We are not inclined to answer your questions." His voice seems to be getting even more robotic and cold.

He takes a breath and gives us snake-like stares. Then continues, "You have been brought here because you are a threat to our operation. We know all about you, where you came from, why you are here. And though we oppose murder we are not afraid to kill you to keep you out of our way."

The female under-dweller to Lottlin's right, shiny metal breasts, tells us, "You are already aware that Jesus Christ is a fake, so your mission has been completed successfully. You must return to your own world now."

"Our mission is not complete," Whyrie says. "The primary goal of our mission is to find Jesus Christ and take him back with us."

"Impossible," says an under-dweller. "He belongs to us."

"We have brought a duplicator," Ni Gonzo says, "We just want a copy of him."

"You can't make a copy," they say.

"The messiah we have created is very special," Lottlin says. "Two of them would make the original only half as special."

"We must still take a look," says Ni Gonzo. "We must see with our own eyes who your Jesus really is."

"Please, we came all this way," says Whyrie, a faked sweetness in her voice. "I've lost a year in search of this man."

The under-dwellers are silent, conversing with each other through angelhair tubes on the table, connected to each other by brain.

"A quick examination is our compromise," says the under-dwellers. "But you must depart without delay once you are through with him."

Ni Gonzo has a crinkled face but nods at them and diverts his eyes.

An under-dweller's smile

ELEVEN

We awake in a landscape of cold purple machinery and whale skeletons. The sky boiling down on us. The sound of waves nearby.

Five under-dwellers stand above us like rubbery sunshade, watching us. All of our clothes have been removed, nude to the sickly environment. We are like sculptures in the alien terrain. Living artwork.

"The sky is the ocean," says the under-dwellers. "Your Atlantic Ocean."

"Where are we then?" Rufus asks.

"We are inside of the reflection in the water," says the under-dwellers.

"Where is your messiah?" asks Ni Gonzo.

They say, "You will return to your own time after you see him."

"Yes, yes, where is he?" Whyrie says, stiff jawed.

A gate of light, similar to our long-distance transports, opens up in the clutter of whale ribs, slicing bones apart.

A man emerges. Slow steps. Awkward posture. He walks to us through the whale bones like it is smooth terrain.

"There he is," the under-dwellers say.

Approaching, our eyes will not blink. We feel

unconscious, like in a dream.

I begin to wonder if I am still real.

When he gets closer, my nerves begin to creep my neck.

Jesus is not a man. What is he?

He is something very wrong.

He is a walking electric corpse, with skin and meat peeling away from his bones. His eyes sewn shut. His beard made of wires and dirt.

The Jesus creature arrives to us, stiff-necked, and raises his shriveled hands to his face to unzip his eyelids. His eyes weren't sewn shut. They were zipped shut. He pulls the zippers and the flesh-flaps open up to reveal black eightball eyes.

And we are all backing away from him.

"What is it?" Whyrie cries.

"It is your messiah," responds the under-dwellers.

"This is an abomination!" Rufus says.

"That is what the Jews said," says the under-dwellers. "That is why they are crucifying him."

"It's impossible," Whyrie says. "He's not a savior. He's a damaged cyborg, a piece of junk."

"He is responsible for the development of your civilization," says the under-dwellers.

"I don't believe you," Whyrie says.

"No," Ni Gonzo grabs my wife's shoulder, shakes her. "No, this is fascinating. This is utterly extraordinary. The idea of a monstrosity such as this being hailed as the Christ is absolutely mind-boggling. Think of how gullible the people of this era must have been to believe in such an absurd piece of work."

The under-dwellers stand motionless, watching with their silvery eyes.

"Look at him!" screams Ni Gonzo. "He's horribly grotesque!"

Ni Gonzo roars out in laughter, points at the under-dwellers, "We came all this way just for this!"

The under-dwellers just stare blank-faced.

"And you people think we shouldn't copy this thing?" Ni Gonzo asks them. "Rufus, make a copy."

"Done," Rufus says, working the controls inside of his head.

The featureless putty man steps to Jesus Christ and gazes into his eightball eyes. Then, slowly, he begins to steal the monster Christ's shape.

The under-dwellers do not object for some reason, standing there, watching their creation being copied right in front of them.

"Aren't you going to try to stop us?" Ni Gonzo

asks, giggling.

But the under-dwellers stay in their places, their wire-hair twisting like medusas.

When the job is done and there are two messiahs on the landscape, the under-dwellers lower their heads and turn away from us, walking to the distance.

The original Jesus Christ dribbles thick black fluids and then staggers back to his gateway.

Loneliness wraps around me as I watch the under-dwellers become floating flames in the distant blue, silent colors flattening into the painting.

"What do we do now?" I ask the scientist-geniuses.

"We go home," they tell me.

TWELVE

Ni Gonzo gathers us around a slimy orange machine with a flat back to use for a table. The air curls around my shoulders, and I stand close to Whyrie.

"Get ready," Ni Gonzo tells us, pulling out the time-travel coin and placing it in the center of the orange slime.

"Will you still love me in the future?" I ask Whyrie.

But she is busy brushing sand away from her stomach.

She isn't smiling, so she must be really happy.

PART FIVE

The Secret of Glog

ONE

We arrive under black water, sucked out of the reflection in the Atlantic Ocean and back to our era. We can no longer breathe, pulling water inside, swimming up but we're unsure which way is up and which way is down, but we take a guess, going fast in one direction, holding Whyrie's bony fingers.

The moon jumps out at me like a yellow turtleshell with red spots. It is surrounded by ice. A big ship is here all ready to pick us up as I'm coughing salt water from my lungs.

But I almost miss the ship, they almost go away without Whyrie and I, like they didn't see us. Perhaps everyone else came earlier through time, called for rescue and were about to go home, guessing we never showed up or drowned.

Whyrie gets their attention with high-pitched screams.

She is pregnant and pissed off.

We are on board, most of us, not sure about everyone. The rescue team yelling words at me but I'm not sure what they all are, wondering if they are speaking another language or perhaps I'm not used to hearing so much English all at once . . .

It has only been a week since we left.

We're taken back to Ocean City brought into protection into a basement somewhere, avoiding the massive crowd that has gathered in the streets, gathered from around the world to see if we have brought Jesus back with us.

They aren't going to like it if they see him. Maybe they'll crucify him again, in this era.

Going down flights of stairs, disoriented from the travel, from almost drowning, hours moving like seconds, eyes flickering.

And I'm not completely conscious until Ni Gonzo's head explodes.

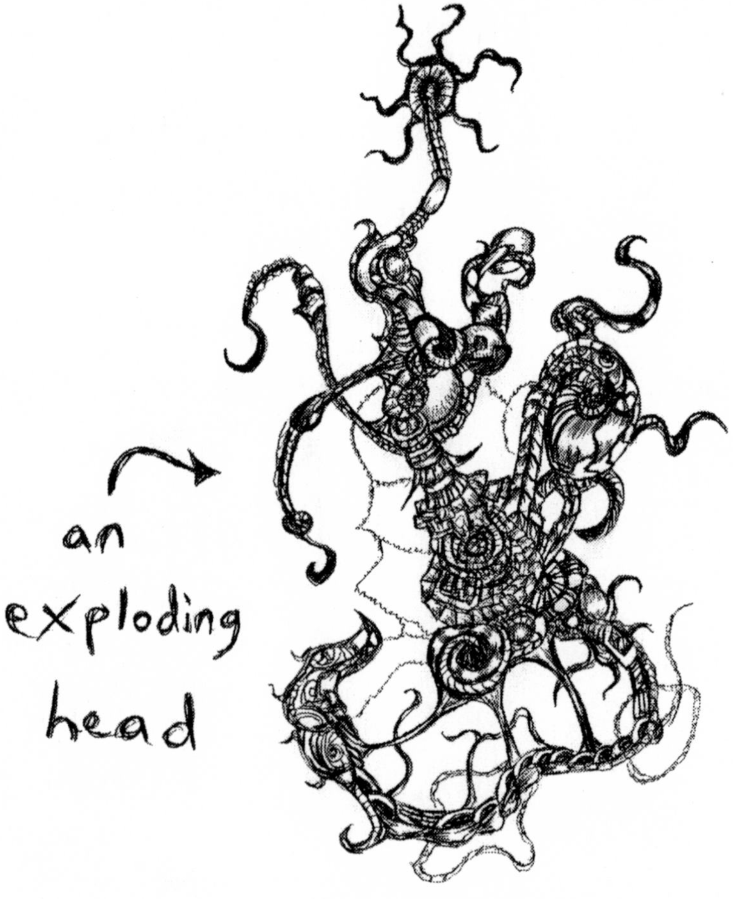
an
exploding
head

TWO

"What's going on?" I scream, Ni Gonzo's skull-pieces splattered on the wall behind us, bloodying the floor with black-red pools.

People are standing in the shadows in front of me, but I can't see them, hiding, angry people.

Another popping sound, Mark's head volcanoes hot goo, his corpse flailing all over the place.

Then again, Rufus, falling back onto some stairs, dripping with ants and foam.

Holding Whyrie's hand, blocking her from the angry ones, shivering lips at them . . .

The slime-hairy Jesus clone just stands there zombie-eyed with chunks of his brain pulsating out of his skull cap.

They must have come for him . . .

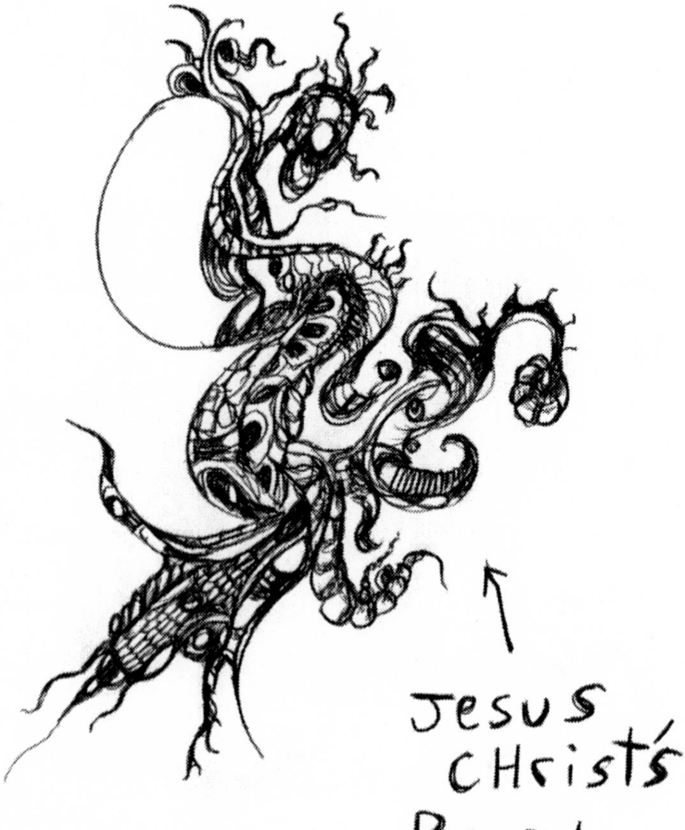

THREE

"They were copies," one of the voices from the shadows mentions, a familiar voice —> Ni Gonzo.

He steps out of the dark. "They weren't really us."

And then his assistants step out of the shadows, Sherry steps out of the shadows, even Jesus Christ Mulligan, and in the back I can see the outline of Whyrie's firm posture, her fists squeezed at me.

"We decided not to go at the last minute," Ni Gonzo continues. "We had copies made of us, perfect clones, but erased their knowledge of creation. They fully believed they were the originals."

Pregnant Whyrie angry-blows at a dangling lock of her fire-green hair and crosses rubbery arms over her belly

Ni Gonzo says to the Whyrie clone, "Copies, as I'm sure you both know, must be destroyed."

"How can I be a clone?" I yell at them.

"You, Cocoan, are not a copy," Ni Gonzo tells me. "You are the real thing."

Sherry says, "We never imagined Whyrie's copy would persuade you into going along. It was a mistake."

"You're the only real human to have ever traveled through time," Rufus says.

I bite the skin around my fingernails.

"What do we do now?" I ask Ni Gonzo.

"That's up to you," he responds.

FOUR

Cloning is illegal these days. The penalty for cloning is very harsh, one of the worst crimes you can commit because people use clones for horrible things anything that requires disposable flesh like wars or prostitution. Clones are just as real as their originals but are treated like pieces of paper, getting used up and thrown out.

"It is up to you," Ni Gonzo says. "Decide."

"How can I do that?" I ask. "They are both the same person."

"Look, Cocoan," Sherry says. "We can't have both of them wandering around, it's too dangerous."

"Let them both live," I tell them. "I'll never be able to forgive myself if either one dies."

"We'll lose everything if they discover we sent copies of ourselves," Mark says.

"We have no problem killing the original if you want us to," Ni Gonzo says. "They are both the same Whyrie, but the world can't have two of them."

"Send us back, then," I tell them. "Back to the Jesus days. We were happy there."

"No," original Whyrie steps out of the shadows. "Let her live until the child is born. After she is destroyed, Cocoan and I will raise it."

"You're willing to do that?" Sherry asks. "Take your clone's child?"

She says, "The child is still my child."

Whyrie clone squeezes my hand, her belly snug

against my back.

Ni Gonzo says, "How did she became pregnant in the first place?"

"Clones aren't supposed to be able to have children," Sherry says.

"Yes, exactly," Ni Gonzo says. "Clones do not have the ability to reproduce."

"That's because I'm not a clone, I'm the original," says the pregnant Whyrie. "I never agreed with sending clones in our place. I wanted to see the past with my own eyes. So I swapped places with her."

"You lying bitch!" Whyrie yells at herself.

"It's the truth," my dirty Whyrie says.

"She's lying," clean Whyrie says, "It's possible for clones to reproduce. You just have to program them correctly. I know how."

"I know I'm the original," pregnant Whyrie says. "Just push the destruct button on your remote. Whichever of us is the fake will be terminated."

"This is true," Ni Gonzo says, holding up the tiny remote.

"No," I cry to pregnant Whyrie. "What if you're the clone? What if your brain explodes like the others?"

"Don't do it," clean Whyrie yells at Ni Gonzo, who holds the remote to her brain. "She's the clone and we all know it. She just doesn't want me to have the child in her. She would rather kill it than allow me to raise it."

"I think I believe the time traveler," Ni Gonzo tells the Whyrie backing into the shadows.

He clicks the button and I close my eyes, a loud pop right inside of my ear, splashings of brain over the walls, sticking to furniture, my legs.

Opening my eyes —> the pregnant Whyrie

smiles at me, kisses my neck.

The clean Whyrie on the floor over there, her skull opened up to the room, warm thoughts emptying to the outside.

"I guess you are the real one," Ni Gonzo tells my dirty Whyrie, exposing pointy gray teeth.

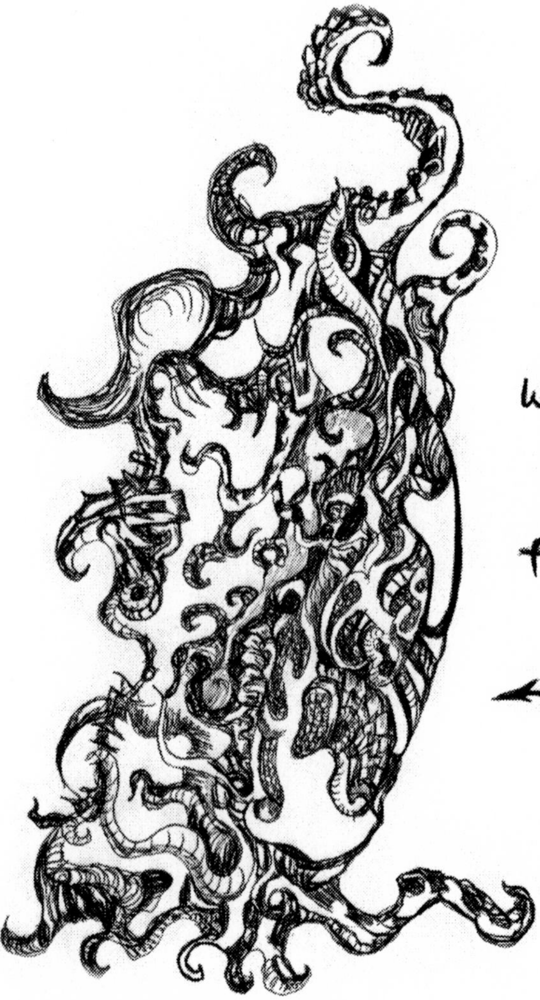

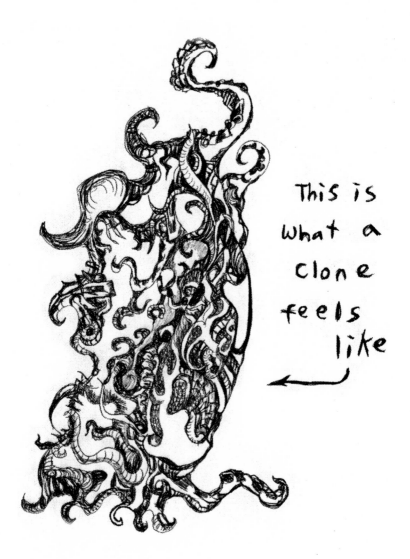

This is what a clone feels like

FIVE

"What do you mean you're not the *real* one?" I yell at Whyrie.

"I'm too smart for them," she tells me, smiling.

"But how? You're pregnant. Your head didn't explode . . ."

"It wasn't hard," she says, snapping her fingers. "It only took a couple phone calls and a little money. Clones switch places with their originals all the time."

I sit down on a glass table and look at the floor for a while. Scrunching the carpeting with my toes.

"Do you still love me?" I ask her. "Even though you're not the real Whyrie?"

"Of course I do." She bends down and kisses me on the nose. "But the real Whyrie didn't. She always hated you."

"But I thought you were both the same person?" I ask.

"Oh, we are," she says. "But the original didn't love you like I do."

SIX

The copy of my wife, who is responsible for the murder of my real wife, her original, who is pregnant with my child, is all over the house —> breaking sculptures and pictures, doing odd dances on the furniture, rubbing her vagina all over things.

"Is something wrong?" I ask, but she does not respond.

It is like there is something wrong with her head something wrong with clones the way they think is mixed up maybe because they are not real, but I like her so much maybe even better than the real Whyrie. I relate to her better. She smiles all the time, though she doesn't always make perfect sense.

"Don't hurt the baby," I tell her, but she isn't listening, jumping around the house . . .

She jumps in front of me, chuckles a little, rubs my face between her legs, and then continues on . . .

SEVEN

Taking the floating bar when it arrives at our house, crowded tonight, people all over the place, and I wanted quiet. I find a chair to sit but it's still packed with screaming ones, ordering a harsh drink to calm me down.

"Cocoan," screams Ni Gonzo from a table across the bar, in the shadowcorners, "Cocoan, come sit with me."

I go to him, his section is less bunched together, more comfortable.

I enter a booth where Ni Gonzo and Rufus and Mark are drinking.

"We have made so much progress since the last time we spoke, Cocoan."

"It's only been a couple weeks," I say.

"We are on the dawn of a new era, my boy," he says.

"Jesus Christ has taught us so much," Rufus yells, chuckling, "He even told us how the world was created."

"How was the world created?" I groggy-ask.

"By a giant fish named Glog," he tells me.

"Glod?" I ask. "Like God with an L?"

"No, *Glog*. It's a giant fish," says Rufus.

"The ancient one," says Ni Gonzo. "The entire world was created for Glog, not mankind. Mankind was created to be its food."

My eyebrows curl.

Ni Gonzo —> "But it does not feed on our flesh, it eats our souls."

"Souls?" I ask.

"After we die, our souls feed Glog."

"The strange part is that there really is a God," Rufus says. "But he exists inside of Glog's stomach. It is the God of Abraham, mentioned in the old testament. It spoke to Moses and the Hebrews. It created mankind."

"I don't get this," I tell them. "What for?"

"Glog's stomach is the Heaven that is written of in the old testament," Ni Gonzo says. "Yahweh, the God in his stomach, is like the illuminated lure of the angler fish, attracting souls to the light so that Glog can gobble them down."

"What about Jesus Christ?" I ask him.

"Jesus Christ is the savior of mankind," Ni Gonzo tells me, and the other two are nodding their heads in my direction.

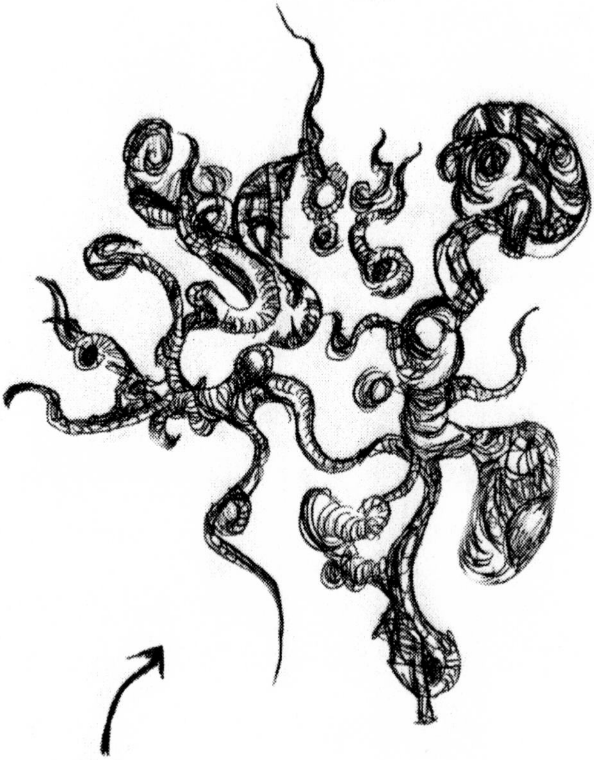

this could
never happen

EIGHT

Ni Gonzo and I, talking about Jesus Christ, walking on the waves outside the city . . .

"He was sent from the future, as I speculated," he tells me. "From a distant future thousands of years from now."

"What for?" I ask.

Ni Gonzo lies down on the cool waves to rock his alcohol buzz back and forth.

"In the future, mankind discovers the secret

of Glog. They find the fish at the bottom of the ocean and kill it with weapons that have yet to be invented. The immortal almighty fish is not as powerful as it thinks." He closes his eyes. "And from its corpse, from its deep black belly, they will find God Himself, sitting in a pool of half-digested souls. A withered fish-fleshed creature. In exchange for His life, He tells the world all of His secrets, all of the secrets of the universe. And then He will give Mankind an idea to save their ancestors from Glog."

Ni Gonzo stares up at the moon and then looks over to me, continues, "God will build them a messiah, which will be Jesus Christ. They will send him back through time to alter the Hebrew religion, so that society changes from its Glog-worshiping state to something brand new, something with a real future."

"But who cares about a messiah?" I tell him, dizzy on the water. "If our souls were meant to be food for a fish, why would we care about saving them?"

"I wondered that, too," he says, jumping from the water.

He continues, "In the future, they will design a man-made Heaven. Something that will put us into ultimate euphoria, for all eternity. A Sutter, they called it. Having power over time, they are able to save souls from thousands of years ago."

I curl into a ball on the waves.

"And the only way people can get into the man-made Heaven is if they accept Jesus Christ into their lives," he continues. "At death, a computer voice will ask them in all languages whether they accept Jesus Christ or not, and if they do their consciousness will enter euphoria instead of wandering the oceans in search for Glog."

"It sounds horrible," I tell him.

"It sounds amazing," Ni Gonzo corrects me.

THE Difference Between WHYrie AND HER Copy

NINE

We're sitting here, goo-rolling in the waves for a while.

"You killed the real Whyrie," I tell Ni Gonzo. "Not her clone."

"I know," Ni Gonzo says.

"How could you know?"

"I can tell the difference between clones and originals. Clones have eyes that shine slightly in the dark."

"Why did you pretend not to know?" I ask.

"I wanted the clone to get away with it. She

outsmarted her original. I respect her."

"She is going insane," I tell him.

"Copies are weaker in the brain than the originals, more susceptible to going insane."

"But what about our child? Is it going to be insane as well?"

"A good question," Ni Gonzo says. "Clones were never allowed to give birth before. We have no idea what will happen."

He wets his face with salt water which repels from his skin. "It should be interesting," he says.

TEN

We walk the waves back to my home, back to Whyrie, Mr. Ni Gonzo curious to see how the clone is doing, curious to see if she is a threat to him a threat she'll give away his practice of cloning and murder of an original Whyrie, I'm sure.

The lights are out in town, a power outage, something rare to the citizens of Ocean City.

Walking the darkness . . .

There is shiny movement up ahead.

"What is that?" I ask Ni Gonzo.

"I'm not sure," he responds.

Then —> an explosion from the buildings, fire mushrooming in the black clouds, debris flying across the water.

Two more explosions, houses crumbling into the ocean. It's like the entire city is getting bombed.

There is a figure in the middle of the chaos, an electric corpse.

"It looks like Jesus," I tell Ni Gonzo.

He squints his eyes.

"Oh, my Glog, you're right," he says.

ELEVEN

We splash into town, running up the road to Jesus Christ.

Most of what we can see of Ocean City has been turned into a wasteland, burning into the sky. People screaming, panicked, as their homes sink to the bottom of the ocean, and Jesus Christ's dark eyes are glowing silver, his arms raised in triumph as the destruction volcanoes overhead, flaming corpses drifting through the streets.

"You son of a bitch," Ni Gonzo screams at the copy of Christ. "What is the meaning of this?"

Christ just stands there, coldly, eyes reflecting fire to Ni Gonzo.

"Why are you doing this?" asks the scientist. "Have you gone insane?"

A bolt of energy stripes through the air from the eyes of Jesus Christ, piercing through Ni Gonzo's chest. Blood oozing, dropping him, a splashing in the street by my legs. He doesn't get back up.

And the copy of Christ shifts his attention to me, eyes lighting up a silvery glow.

"The afterlife is bliss," says the Christ. "Believe in me."

And his eyes become wide with fire, bright yellow, blocking out the dark dead city behind him, and I can feel the bolt of light itching to strike me down as it did Ni Gonzo, itching to put me into the box of euphoria for all eternity.

My eyes close shut, hoping my death comes

as easy as it did the first time.

A loud popping noise, and my eyes jerk open, witnessing the copy of Jesus Christ dropping into the water, its skull shattered into flames, silver goo like mercury oozing out swirl ing the salt water.

Beyond the road, Ni Gonzo's assistant Rufus stands on the water, watching me. He holds the termination remote in his hand.

"The Christ must not have copied properly," Rufus yells to me. "He must have malfunctioned."

I drop to the water, curl into a ball.

The water carries me back and forth. My brain becomes smooth like the waves. I try to suck the water into my mouth but it repels against my lips.

"Are you okay?" Rufus calls to me.

My eyes close, rolling to the back of my head.

"Are you okay?" Rufus calls again.

When he doesn't get a response, he stays silent, pausing.

I open my eyes and see him walking into the burning city, slow smoke around him.

"I'm not okay," I say, but he us too far to hear, the water surface breaking, bouncing away from my words. "Nothing is okay."

I reach to my hipbone and tap the button in the flesh there, releasing my water legs.

All the air goes out of my lungs, pressed tightly into that ball. I sink into the water, down into the ocean, the sick world of undead fish. My head spins. Peaceful hums all around me, wondering what euphoria is like . . .

TWELVE

Trudging back home, my head rotten and spongy, crashing over the waves.

The lights in town have re-illuminated, giving me a clear picture of corpses floating in the streets, sad reflections on the water, sickness in my ear . . .

Most everyone in the neighborhood is dead.

A rescue party is sure to arrive soon, but has yet to find this place. Perhaps the rescuers are among the corpses.

In my house —> the walls are covered in

blood, painted swirl-drawings.

All of our belongings have been torn apart, ground into the carpeting, muck drizzling from the stairs.

The side of the house is starting to catch on fire. A loud cracking noise and smoke snails up the wall like ghosts.

"Whyrie?"

I'm stepping up, squishy sounds from the bedroom, lights bright all around me, zebra-shadows, lamps have been violently rearranged.

Chunks of mess slime my feet.

"Whyrie?"

"I'm over here," the clone says.

"What are you doing there?" I ask the Whyrie copy.

"Waiting for you," she says.

I come to her, see her lying on the bathroom floor, blood-smudged face and shrunken belly, a silent ball of meat in her lap.

"It came early," she says.

"What did?" I ask.

"It's so beautiful . . ." says Whyrie's clone.

She holds the pile of flesh up to me, all red, featureless skin, not even limbs, a meat ball crawling with dark blood vessels.

Fire crawls up the staircase.

"What is this?" I ask, watching it squish around in her arms.

"Our baby," she says, smiling.

"Where is the head?" I ask.

"It's coming," she says excitedly, pointing at the meat ball. "Look!"

Staring closely at the blob of putty-skin, I watch

as a mirror image of my face forms out of the meat, the entire body becomes a copy of my head.

Just my head.

"There he is," Whyrie clone says. "Isn't he beautiful?"

The putty-head coos at me.

"More than I imagined . . ." I tell her.

I smile at Whyrie, smoke pouring into the room, and she smiles back.

She gives me our baby and I hug my head/infant to my chest, blood leaking onto the floor.

"Things will be much better from now on," she tells me.

"Much, much better," I tell her.

Closing my eyes and escaping to my own private godless heaven.

. . .

heavan
emotions

“There is no truth. There is only perception.”

- Gustave Flaubert

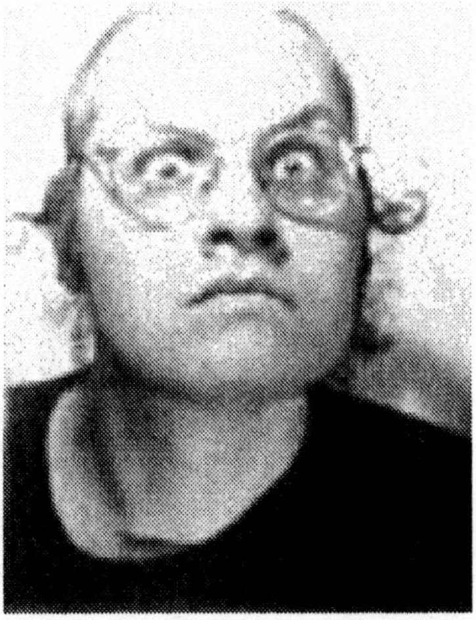

ABOUT THE AUTHOR

Carlton Mellick III has published eight books, has written twenty-seven, and completes nearly four new books each year. He has had over 80 short stories published in magazines, chapbooks, and anthologies, including THE YEAR'S BEST FANTASY AND HORROR 16. His first published novel, SATAN BURGER, is becoming a cult favorite among fringe lit and alternative culture circles, and has been the #1 bestselling horror novel at Amazon.com. He lives in Portland, OR, where he mows lawns made of fingers and toes.

Visit him online at http://www.avantpunk.com

AVANT PUNK

WWW.AVANTPUNK.COM

BOOKS BY CARLTON MELLICK III

If you like your fiction on the strange side, check out more titles by Carlton Mellick III. As an underground author, his books can only be special ordered at local bookstores or purchased through online retailers such as www.amazon.com. If you'd like this to change, please ask your bookstores and libraries to carry future CM3 books.

Teeth and Tongue Landscape

Carlton Mellick III's fleshscape novella
(Published with Angel Scene by Richard Kadrey)

In a world made out of meat, a socially-obsessive monophobic man finds himself to be the last human being on the face of the planet. Desperate for social interaction, he explores the landscape of flesh and blood, teeth and tongue, trying to befriend any strange creature or community that he comes across.

"This generation's Vonnegut!" - Vincent W. Sakowski
Satan Burger
an anti-novel
Carlton Mellick III

Satan Burger

Carlton Mellick III's debut novel

"This generation's Vonnegut!" - Vincent Sakowski

"An utterly fascinating, inventive and oftentimes hilarious read." - Margaret Marr, AAS REVIEWS

Absurd philosophies, dark surrealism, and the end of the human race . . .

God hates you. All of you. He closed the gates of Heaven and wants you to rot on Earth forever. Not only that, he is repossesing your souls and feeding them to a large vagina-like machine called the Walm - an interdimensional doorway that brings His New Children into the world. He loves these new children, but He doesn't love you. They are more interesting than you. They are beautiful, psychotic, magical, sex-crazed, and deadly. They are turning your cities into apocalyptic chaos, and there's nothing you can do about it ...

Featuring: a narrator who sees his body from a third-person perspective, a man whose flesh is dead but his body parts are alive and running amok, an overweight messiah, the personal life of the Grim Reaper, lots of classy sex and violence, and a motley group of squatter punks that team up with the devil to find their place in a world that doesn"t want them anymore.

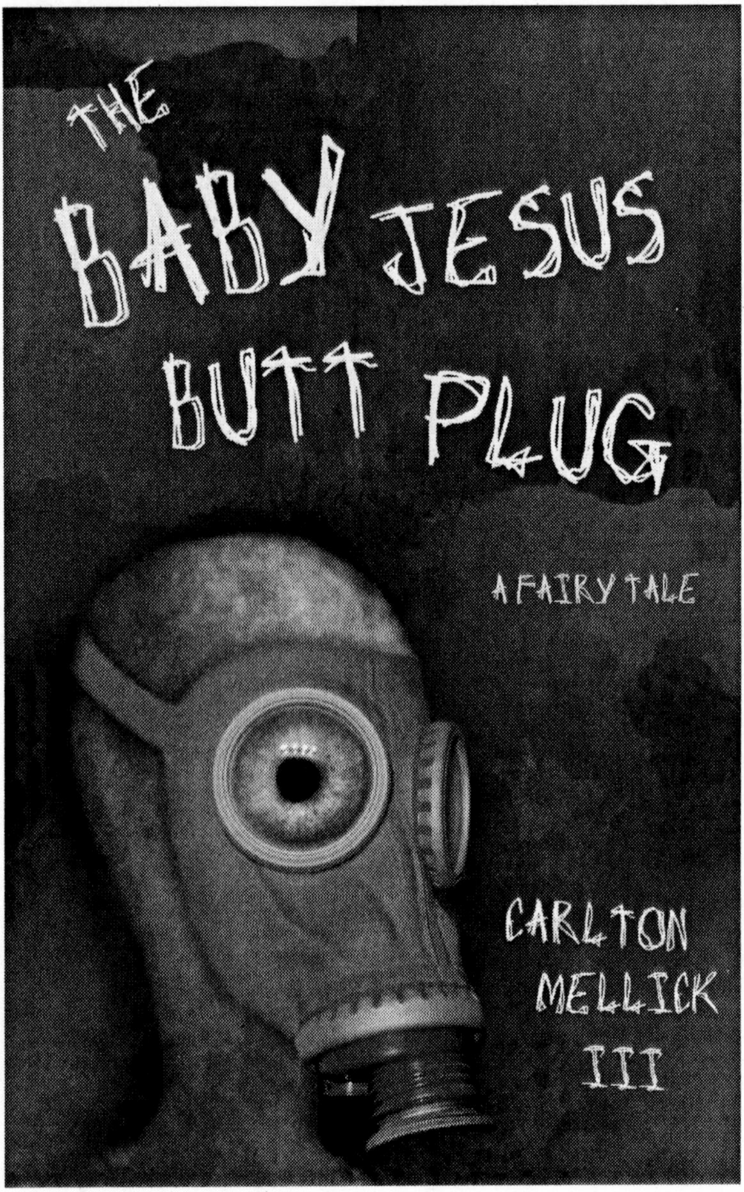
THE
BABY JESUS
BUTT PLUG
A FAIRY TALE
CARLTON
MELLICK
III

Baby Jesus Butt Plug

"Reading Carlton Mallick III's BABY JESUS BUTT PLUG is like hopping into an LSD-filled time machine with David Cronenberg, William Burroughs, J.G. Ballard, Philip K. Dick, and George Romero at the controls. This tale of office drones and disposable clones is a splatterpunk odyssey, a cautionary tale of corporate omnipotence, and a possible blueprint of the future of the nuclear family. Touching, poignant, horrorific, nightmarish, and beautiful all at the same time, BABY JESUS BUTT PLUG is the work of an uncompromising visionary who lances the boil of his seething imagination with the tip of his pen . . ."

- Trent Haaga, star of
Terror Firmer, Troma's Edge TV,
and co-writer of Citizen Toxie

Razor Wire
Pubic Hair
an anti-novel of the future by Carlton Mellick III

Razor Wire Pubic Hair

Carlton Mellick III's illustrated psycho-sexual fairy tale

A multi-gender screwing toy who is purchased by a razor dominatrix and brought into her nightmarish worlds of bizarre sex and mutilation.

"Razor Wire Pubic Hair is freaky, funny, brutal, techno-noir, limit-situation stuff set in a bad-dream future that's ultimately a metaphor for a present-day journey into the relentless nature of desire and the delicious permeability of gender. Somewhere right this second David Cronenberg, H. R. Giger, a young David Lynch, and a wizened Doug Rice are smiling because they know something extraordinary has just birthed in the Arizonan Desert of the Real. Read this, duck, and cover." - Lance Olsen, author of Freaknest

"I would call this a happy world to live in, with only brute body modified women and hermaphroditic sex toys, but I suppose constantly fighting off hordes of murderous rapists and needing to deposit your womb in a machine to make an ugly squishy baby would be a drawback." - Jasmine Sailing, editor/publisher Cyber-Psychos AOD

"Carlton Mellick III takes readers on an ultra-bizarre sexual nightmare with his novella 'Razor Wire Pubic Hair.' He blends a surreal landscape into a dark, hopeless future, creating disturbing, yet thought-provoking sequences of events that ultimately delve into horrors of lust and sex. This novella is a page turner of strange proportions. Your mind will twist into the shadowy points between eroticism and insanity, quickly addicted to the author's avant-guarde style. Mellick is a bizarre visionary, and this novella showcases his talented prose and twisted imaginings." - Shane Ryan Staley, author of I'll Be Damned

"Naked Lunch meets Re-animator during the zombie apocalypse."
The
STEEL BREAKFAST ERA
by
Carlton Mellick III
with tattoos by Pooch

The Steel Breakfast Era

Carlton Mellick III's surreal zombie novella
(Published as a split with author Simon Logan)

A nightmarishly absurd story that is like "RE-ANIMATOR" meets "NAKED LUNCH" during the zombie apocalypse.

Plot: The living dead conquered the Earth almost a century ago, leaving only small isolated communities of survivors spread across the shattered-earwig landscape. One such community has been locked away in a New York City high-rise. Breeding like cockroaches for many generations, their civilization has almost completely deteriorated into a mess of insane ones and those infested with parasites that mutate flesh into steel-string sculptures. There is nothing to live for, no chance for hope. Except for one man, not yet effected by the parasites, who finds hope after he creates a wife out of the human body parts that litter the hallways and gets rescued by a group of zombie-shredding warriors from Japan (where the citizens have evolved into anime-like mechazoid characters). This tattoo-illustrated avant-garde novel is rising cult author, Carlton Mellick III, at his darkest and most horrific.

"THE STEEL BREAKFAST ERA is a feverishly bizarre journey through a world where flesh has taken on the quality of living poetry. Written in a first-person present-tense immediacy that gives you no time to question the strange events as they unfold, cmIII's style describes technology-as-magic in a straight-forward manner that hypnotizes as it informs. How he manages to infuse even the most grotesque imagery of twisted and broken limbs with a strangely erotic charge is something to be admired. Trippy in the extreme, compellingly told and resolutely modern in the storytelling, this is a book well worth owning if you want to keep an eye on the future of the genre." - Scooter McCrae, writer/director of SHATTER DEAD and SIXTEEN TONGUES

Forthcoming books
by Carlton Mellick III
(2004/2005)

The Ocean of Lard
(w/ Kevin L. Donihe)

The Menstruating Mall

Punk Land

Sex and Death in
Television Town

The Cockroach People

Ugly Heaven

The Eyeball Wizard's
Toy Cunt

Young Adolf Hitler

Sea of the Patchwork Cats

Skinhead Girls

For more authors of the surreal and bizarre

check out:

www.ERASERHEADPRESS.com

Printed in the United States
25944LVS00002B/112-117